Y0-DWN-594

[handwritten inscription, partially legible]

To the
Critterden,
Choose not to look
back on your life saying
"I wish I could have be
"I must." on - I could have done
To God Be the Glory!
able to say doing,
- I am doing!
Martha J. Ross-...
www.jirehpublishe...

Awakenings

Awakenings
by Martha J. Ross-Rodgers

Jireh Publishers

Awakenings. © 1998 by Martha J. Ross-Rodgers. Printed and bound in the United States of America. Published by Jireh Publishers, P.O. Box 99003, Norfolk, VA 23509-9003. Edited by Charizza S. S. Rodgers.

Publisher's Cataloging in Publication
(Prepared by Quality Books Inc.)

Rodgers, Martha J. Ross, 1958-
    Awakenings/Martha J. Ross-Rodgers.--Rev. 2nd ed.
    p. cm.
    ISBN 0-9653197-0-9

1. Family--Fiction. 2. Interpersonal relationships--Fiction.
I. Title
PS3568.O34818A96 1998   813'.54
                       QBI96-40271

Attention: Quantity discounts are available on bulk purchases of this book for educational training purposes, fund rasing, or gift giving. A workbook designed to be used in conjunction with Awakenings can be included. For information contact: Jireh Publishers, P.O. Box 99003, Norfolk, Virginia 23509-9003

How to Contact the Author:
Martha J. Ross-Rodgers speaks to many businesses, associations, churches and nonprofit organizations nationwide. Inquiries about her availability for speaking should be directed to her at the address below. Readers of this book are also encouraged to contact the author with comments.

Martha J. Ross-Rodgers
Jireh Publishers
P.O. Box 99003
Norfolk, Virginia 23509-9003
(757) 855-6307

ACKNOWLEDGMENTS

First and foremost, I would like to give thanks to God. I would also like to thank my husband, Reginald, who has always encouraged me to be the best I can be. He has been a rock throughout our years together. I would also like to thank my two daughters, Charizza and Gina, who are a source of inspiration. I give thanks to my father, L.D. Ross, and my beloved mother, Ida Ross, who passed away April 1, 1995. To everyone else I failed to name—I *do* thank you and appreciate you.

MARTHA J. ROSS-RODGERS

LETTER FROM THE AUTHOR

Dear Readers:

One of the main reasons why I wrote <u>Awaken-ings,</u> is that there are too many people sitting on the sidelines of life. They sit there watching things happen in other peoples lives, instead of making things happen in their own lives.

I believe that each individual is born with at least one talent or gift, that is to be used for the benefit of mankind.

"Why," I wondered, "do so many people come to the end of their lives never having done the things that they wanted to?"

The main purpose of <u>Awakenings</u> is to encour-age you to go after your dreams. Your dreams can turn into reality.

Choose not to look back on your life, saying "I wish" or "I could have." Be able to say "I have done" and "I am doing."

MARTHA J. ROSS-RODGERS

TABLE OF CONTENTS

CHAPTER 1

A Taste of the Real World

I t was a beautiful day. The sun was shining and the birds were chirping. Inside the gray house on Banks Street, Betty slowly got out of bed. Looking out her window, she didn't notice the brightly shining sun, nor did she hear the birds chirping. Betty heard the creaking of pipes as her mom turned on the water downstairs. She heard mice scurrying about for food. She saw the familiar faces of people standing under the big oak tree, drowning their disappointments with a bottle of liquor.

There was Albert who had hoped to be a famous basketball player. He had spent all his waking hours practicing on the basketball court. School never was important to him. He believed that he didn't have to know how to read well to put a basketball through the hoop. He could however, write his name well—for he eagerly waited to sign the million-dollar contract that never came.

Standing behind Albert was Louise. Louise had once dreamed of becoming a doctor. Yes, she had big dreams! But her dreams were crushed, little by little, as each of her four children were born. Now at the age of 24, she drinks herself to another world; a world where she's the person she so desperately wants to become.

The last person in the oak tree trio was Johnny. Johnny once had big dreams of becoming a singer. School was secondary to him. He used to spend his time learning new songs and dance steps. He knew that he had lots of talent and that he could make it in the entertainment field. Now he spends his days singing to the music on his radio.

Even though Betty couldn't hear their conversation, she knew the content of it. She had heard it so many times before—people talking about what they *could have done* with their lives. They would say, "I could have been successful, but . .." Yes, there was always the word "but."

Betty slowly turned away from the window. Seeing all the familiar faces by the oak tree and thinking about her future made her feel disillusioned, even though she was only 15 years old. She was very determined that she would be successful in her life. She had plans for becoming so much more than those "I could have been" people standing under the oak tree.

"But how?" Betty wondered. She knew that money was the key. If she dropped out of school, she could get a head start on making money. Why should she waste her time by finishing high school? She had heard the familiar stories that education was power, but she didn't believe it. *Money* was power, not education. She didn't have to get an education, but she could surely make lots of money.

"Grown-ups," she thought, "only tell kids that getting a good education is important to scare them into doing their best in school."

"Well," Betty thought, "it won't work on me." Betty really didn't hate school. In fact, she enjoyed some of her classes. Her favorite subject was science. She loved to figure out how things worked. She remembered how excited she was the day her science teacher, Mrs. Daniels, praised the experiment she did on gravity. Mrs. Daniels was always telling her that she had the potential to do great things for the scientific world. "Hogwash," Betty would mumble low enough that her teacher couldn't hear her. She believed that money—and plenty of it—was her ticket to success, not science. She could hardly wait until she reached the legal age so she could drop out of school.

Just then, Betty heard her mom call for her to come and eat breakfast. Quickly, she put on her clothes and hurried down to the kitchen where her mom was stirring a pot of grits on the stove. She turned as Betty entered the room and said, "You know you have to go to school today. So why are you taking your time this morning?"

"Mom," said Betty, "I really don't want to go to school today. I can't wait until I can drop out of school. I would like to get a job working with you. Then we can make more money so we can buy more of the things we need."

Betty's mom looked down at her calloused hands. She too, had dropped out of high school to pursue what she thought was the quickest way to riches. For all of her working years, she had worked as a maid doing for other people what she once dreamed someone would be doing for her. Tears welled up in her eyes as she thought about the same fate awaiting Betty. She wanted what any mother wanted for her child—only the best. She would just have to teach Betty that dropping out of school wasn't the answer.

"But how?" she wondered.

Betty's mom slowly turned back to stirring the grits on the stove. She thought about her mother who had tried to make her complete high school. But she was not interested. She was in love and wanted to get married. The young couple had dreams of conquering the world. Yes, they thought they would have it all. She fought back the bitter tears as she thought about everything that had happened in her life. She ended up pregnant and unmarried at the young age of 15, struggling for her survival and her child's. She knew that forcing Betty to attend school would defeat the purpose of teaching her that the easiest way out was not necessarily the best. She knew that she would have to *show* Betty the truth and guide her into accepting the hard facts of reality.

Turning slowly toward Betty, she asked, "How would you like to work with me a couple of hours during the evening?" Without waiting for a response, her mom continued, "Then you can see exactly what I do. You'll get paid the same amount I do. However, you'll have to pay some of the household expenses, for that is part of the real world."

Betty was so excited that she forgot to ask her mom how much she would have to pay. It was easier than she thought it would be to persuade her mom to allow her to start working.

Betty could hardly wait until school was over that day. She thought about all the things that she would buy with the money she made. She ran home from school and caught the bus with her mom to her job.

As the bus left the inner city and entered the suburban area, Betty felt as if she would burst wide open with excitement. The houses she saw were like the ones she had seen in magazines.

"One day," she thought to herself as she saw the beautiful fenced houses, "I'll live in a pretty house like one of these."

Soon, Betty and her mom arrived at their stop. They got off the bus and quickly walked up the street to a red brick house with pretty flowers and shrubs around it. Betty was awestruck at the size of the house. It was the largest she had ever seen, and the scent from the flowers was breathtaking.

Betty's mom rang the doorbell. A tall, distinguished looking black woman by the name of Mrs. Bell answered the door and ushered them into the foyer. Betty stood there with her mouth slightly open staring at Mrs. Bell. She could hardly believe that a woman of her race actually owned this place. Yes, she had read and seen pictures about well-to-do black people, but to actually stand there with one was like a dream.

After they hung their jackets in the hall closet, Mrs. Bell began to give them instructions on what needed to be done. After Mrs. Bell left, Betty's mom gave Betty a list of chores that she wanted her to do. Betty carefully looked at her list. She thought it was an awful lot to do, but the money she would earn would make it all worthwhile in the end.

Betty's last chore was to dust the books in the den. It seemed as if there were hundreds and hundreds of books.

"What would a person want with all these books?"

wondered Betty, talking aloud to herself as she dusted.

Just then, Betty saw some science books. She took one down from the shelf to look through it quickly. Betty found the book so interesting that she sat down in the big leather chair by the bookcase. The chair was so soft and comfortable that she completely forgot she was there to do a job.

Time passed. Suddenly, Betty heard someone speaking softly in front of her. Standing before her was Mrs. Bell. Betty jumped up from the leather chair, apologizing for reading when she was supposed to have been working.

"There's no need to apologize. I see that you like science," said Mrs. Bell as she picked up the science book, stroking the cover with her well-manicured hands.

"Yes," Betty responded. "Science is my favorite subject in school."

"What are you planning on doing after high school?" asked Mrs. Bell.

"Well," Betty smugly said, "I'm not planning on finishing school. I'd prefer to get a job as soon as possible."

"I see," said Mrs. Bell with a twinkle in her eyes, for Betty's mom had told her beforehand why she was bringing Betty to work there.

"Mrs. Bell," said Betty with a puzzled look on her face, "why do you have so many books?"

"I love to read," answered Mrs. Bell. "I'm a scientist, so I like to keep abreast of all the new theories."

"Uh, uh," murmured Betty, "That's nice, but...

well, I presume you had to go to college for that. But as far as I'm concerned, education doesn't guarantee you a good job."

"Very true," explained Mrs. Bell. "There are no guarantees that you'll get a good job after finishing college. But knowledge is power. It's power to be able to read well, and to comprehend what you've read. It's power to understand your finances; otherwise, other people will be in control of your money. Yes, knowledge is definitely power. The more you know about the intricacies of living, the better off you'll be."

"Well, I know what I want, and I believe that I can do it without completing high school," said Betty confidently, as she gathered her dusting equipment to leave the room.

As Betty was leaving the den, her mom approached her with their jackets so they could prepare to go home. Betty did not realize just how tired she was until they boarded the bus. Nor did she realize, until then, just how hard her mom had to work to earn a living. In spite of her tiredness, she was excited about earning her own money. She could hardly wait until Friday when her mom got paid so she could get her share of the money that her mom had promised her.

"Only four more days until Friday," she thought excitedly as she started the countdown.

The next morning, Betty quickly got out of bed and dressed for school. She didn't hear the creaking of the pipes or the scurrying of the mice. She was really excited, for each morning was a day closer to Friday.

After she finished eating her breakfast, she got her book bag and headed for school. This time though, she didn't go directly to school. She stopped by the oak tree to talk to Albert, Louise, and Johnny. She was so happy that she wanted to tell everyone.

"Guess what?" cried Betty. "I started working with my mom yesterday. She's going to pay me on Friday and I'm going to have lots of money. When I get old enough, I'll be able to drop out of school and make even more money."

Louise snickered, "Little girl, you got a whole lot of growing up to do. Do you really believe you're going to make a lot of money by dropping out of school and being a maid like your mom? How do you expect to live?"

Albert, Louise, and Johnny burst out laughing. "Yeah," mocked Albert, "Little girl, we'll reserve you a space under this oak tree. If you drop out of school, you'll end up no different from us. Right now, you think you have all the answers. Just wait and see. You'll be back, Betty."

Betty ran from them as fast as she could. She could hear them laughing at her. Albert's parting words, "You'll be back," kept echoing in her head.

"I'll show them," Betty angrily said aloud. They were losers and she was determined not to follow their path. She was determined to be a winner.

The next three days of work proceeded just like the first day. Each evening, Betty came home so exhausted, she could barely wait until she got into bed. Finally, Friday came. Betty was so excited that she ignored her aching body. That evening after work, her mom would give her the share of money she had earned.

Time seemed to be at a standstill, but finally evening came. Betty could hardly wait until she and her mom got home from work. Finally, they arrived home.

Betty's mom said, "Well, Betty, here's the share of the money you've earned. You worked very hard this week and I'm very proud of you. You worked 20 hours, so I owe you $103. Your social security deduction is $7.88. Now you have to pay me the expenses that I told you about before. You owe me $20 for food, $20 for room and board, and $8 for bus fare. The rest is yours."

Betty looked at her mom in amazement. She had focused so much on her gross earnings that she never once thought about her expenses. Disappointment rose in her as she realized that she had worked so hard for only $47.12 left.

"This is not fair," screamed Betty. "It's just not fair!"

Betty's mom replied, "I know this doesn't seem fair to you, Betty, but this is reality—the real world. So many times I have heard you talk about having plenty of money. How are you going to do it, Betty? Quitting school is not the answer. So many young people believe like you that going to school is a waste of time. It's not, Betty. It's not!"

Betty's mom knew that this was really her golden opportunity to teach her daughter a crucial lesson on the importance of gaining an education. With intensity in her voice, she continued, "Be all that you can be, Betty. Don't settle for less. Yes, I know you think you have all the answers and you can't lose. Wake up, Betty! I too, thought I had all the answers. I too, felt that I was wasting my time in school. Now here I am cleaning other people homes, trying to make ends meet. No, an education is no guarantee, Betty, that you will get a good job. But it's a start in the right direction. Look at me! Just look at me!"

Betty looked at her mom as if she were seeing her for the first time. She saw the premature lines of aging on her face, her calloused hands and the tiredness in her eyes. Then she thought about Mrs. Bell's well manicured hands. She could hear the jeers of Albert, Louise, and Johnny as she ran from them. She knew then that her mother had done this to help her understand that quitting school was not the answer. She knew then that the paths she chose early in life could affect her entire life. She knew then that she would not only complete high school, but that she would be the best student that she could be. She knew then that the big oak tree would never be a part of her future. For Betty, that moment was a new beginning—an awakening.

CHAPTER 2

A Change Has Come Over Me

W ell, it would be nice to say that Betty would achieve everything that she desired with out any obstacles in her way, but we all know that such smooth sailing happens only in fairy tales. Real life involves continued hard work and lots of determination. The question now is: Does Betty really have what it takes or is this a passing phase in which she will succumb to defeat?

Betty woke up the next morning feeling as if she had been reborn. She was ready to take on the whole world. Now she was feeling really good about her life. Finishing high school and going to college were not such farfetched dreams anymore. Yes, she knew she must start taking advanced courses, but she was willing to do whatever was necessary to make up for lost time.

After breakfast, she hurried off to school. She wanted to arrive before school started so she could talk to her career counselor, Mr. Merman. She arrived earlier than he did that morning and had to wait about 10 minutes for him to arrive. While she was waiting, she thought about what she would say to him. She knew that she had not previously worked to her full potential, but she felt that she deserved a chance to now.

"Oh well," she said to herself. "This should be easy. I just have to convince him that I'm capable."

Before she could think of what she would say, in walked Mr. Merman, a tall man with small beady eyes.

"Hello," he said in a raspy voice. "How can I help you this morning?"

"My name is Betty Tate," answered Betty, "and I have come to talk to you about taking one advanced course this semester."

"Let me get your school record," replied Mr. Merman, "and see what prior courses you've taken."

Mr. Merman went to his file cabinet and got Betty's record. He looked through her record briefly and said, "Betty, from your school record, I see that you're not doing well in your regular courses. Your grades for last semester are a *C-* in literature, a *D* in algebra II, an *A* in earth science, and a *C-* in world history. What makes you think you'll be able to start taking advanced courses now?"

"Mr. Merman," Betty explained, "I know that I haven't worked to my full potential, but now I want too. I have to start taking advanced courses now because I want to win a scholarship to college."

Mr. Merman laughed in a loud, raspy voice. He retorted, "Many students like you come into my office on a whim, trying to assure me that they have done a turnabout. I'm going to tell you exactly what I tell them. Betty, you are not able to handle advanced courses. Sure, right now you think you can, but these courses require work—lots of it. You are very gung ho now, but just wait until the excitement dies down. I can't stop you, but I can advise you on what I think is best for you. You just have to see for yourself that you're not capable. You can come back any time and drop this course."

"Mr. Merman," Betty firmly said, "I can't speak for the other students who have failed, but I can speak for myself. This is not a passing whim. You'll see."

After Betty signed up for calculus, she sat on the stoop on the side of the school. She had a few minutes before the first period bell rang. Now she felt as if she needed some time to herself to think about Mr. Merman's negative reaction to her. Unfortunately, she had assumed that other people would believe in her abilities after hearing her explanation. But she just didn't realize the impact her past would have on her present. Simply saying she had changed just wasn't enough—she had to prove herself.

Just then, the warning bell rang for class. Betty had switched her literature class to another period so she could take calculus during the first period. Even though school had been in session for a week, the calculus course had just started because of a lack of students.

Betty walked down the long hallway until she found room #105. She went in and sat in the first seat directly in front of the teacher's desk. As the first bell rang, the calculus teacher, Miss Becker, walked in.

"Good morning class," she said. "My name is Miss Becker. As you all know, this is Calculus. There is a lot of hard work involved in this course. I expect each of you to do your best. I am really glad to see that I have 10 students in this course. Students avoid this course because they view it as difficult, as something that is above their capacity to learn."

As if to reassure her 10 students that they each had the capacity to learn, Miss Becker said encouragingly, "Each week we will learn an inspirational verse. I want each of you to memorize each verse, until it becomes a part of you. The verse for this week is:

> *I am capable* of learning anything I put my mind to.
>
> Yes, I may have to work harder than others; but I am capable of succeeding.
>
> I don't need to dwell on my failures.
>
> I need to focus on improving my present.
>
> *I can succeed."*

"The contrast between Miss Becker and Mr. Merman is quite striking," Betty thought as she wrote the verse in her folder. Even though Miss Becker had never viewed her school record, she was saying that her past failures really did not matter, that she was capable of being successful in her endeavors.

Betty concentrated very hard during the rest of the class. "There are so many formulas to learn to apply," Betty thought, "more than I ever imagined." She definitely had to go over her notes that night. At the end of the class, Miss Becker told the class that they would have their first quiz that coming Thursday.

Negative thoughts started going through Betty's mind as she walked to her next class: "Suppose I flunk the test on Thursday. Maybe I got into something I can't handle."

By the end of the school day, Betty felt completely overwhelmed. She had a lot of catching up to do in her courses—plus, she had to prepare herself for the calculus test.

While walking home from school, she thought about how she was going to manage to do well in all of her courses.

"Well," she thought; "I just have to put myself on a schedule. When I get home, I'll write down everything I did prior to quitting work with mom. Then I can make some changes."

After Betty got home from school, she wrote down what she normally did after school. She was quite surprised to see that she spent only 30 minutes doing homework, while she spent the rest of the time looking at television and being with her best friend, Gabby. On reflection, she also discovered that she never studied for an exam until the night before.

"Well," she said, "I definitely have to make some major changes."

She decided to allot herself 30 minutes per night watching television and 30 minutes with Gabby each school day. During the weekend, she could spend more time with Gabby and could also watch more television. But her studies had to be her first priority. She also decided to spend three hours doing homework and reviewing notes she took in class daily. Then, if she didn't understand something, she could ask the teacher the next day. This would make it easier for her, especially before exams. Then she wouldn't have to cram at the last minute.

She knew that it would be difficult at first to stick to her plan. But she had made her choice and was determined to stick with it. She knew that, like any habit, it would become easier as time passed. Also, she knew that Gabby would understand, for they had been best friends since kindergarten. Betty smiled to herself as she thought about the pact that they had made to each other to always be best friends. Since kindergarten, they had done nearly everything together. In fact, they were called the "Bobbsey Twins," for seldom was one seen without the other.

"Oops!" thought Betty. "I've had so much on my mind that I forgot to wait for Gabby so that we could walk home from school together. Huh, I will go over her house now."

Betty left her mom a note and headed out the door. She had a short walk, for Gabby lived only five houses down from her. She walked up the steps and rang the doorbell. After the third ring, Gabby finally answered the door. Excitedly, Betty started telling Gabby about everything that had happened to her. But suddenly Betty stopped talking. The expression on Gabby's face was one she had never seen before.

"Gabby," cried Betty, "is there something wrong? Why are you looking at me like that?"

"What about us?" protested Gabby. "Remember, we're supposed to be best friends. Now you're telling me that you're setting a limit on how much time we spend together each day. I really don't understand why you want to take advanced courses anyway."

Gabby reflected for a while and then began to laugh. "You are no different from me, yet here you're trying to be someone you're not. You're changing, Betty, and I really don't like what I see," she added angrily.

"Gabby," Betty responded in a soft but firm tone, "I really didn't expect this reaction from you. As best friends, we should want the best for each other. Just what does the word 'friend' mean to you? What are you afraid of, Gabby? You wouldn't be so angry with me if I weren't trying to make something out of my life. I see now that we have different definitions of the word *friend*."

Betty agonized as she realized that a wall of separation was now rising between her and Gabby, but she felt compelled to take a stand. "I still want you as a friend, Gabby," Betty said, "but I won't let you belittle my efforts to better myself. If you're going to hinder my progress, then we must part. You see, I've come a long way to the point where I believe—I mean, *really* believe—in myself. I will not let you take this away from me. It's your choice, Gabby. You know how I feel about it. When you make your decision, let me know. You know where you can find me."

Betty turned and quickly walked out of Gabby's house. She didn't want Gabby to see the tears that had welled up in her eyes, but as soon as she got far enough from Gabby's house, her tears began to flow freely.

"Why?" she sobbed. "Why? Is what I'm doing worth losing my best friend? Is it?"

The pain she felt was almost unbearable. She knew that she had just lost her best friend. When she got to her house, she blindly fumbled for her house key. She felt so emotionally drained by the time she got inside her bedroom that she flopped on her bed. She needed some time alone to think about everything that had happened.

Betty drifted off to sleep. When she woke up, it was dark inside her room.

"I must have slept for hours," she thought to herself, as she heard the clicking of the key in the door downstairs. "Mom is home now. I really need to talk to her."

Betty went into the bathroom and washed her face and brushed her teeth. Then she went downstairs to greet her mom. Her mom immediately noticed that her eyes were red and puffy.

With concern in her voice, she inquired, "What's wrong, Betty?" After Betty finished telling her mom everything that had happened, she felt as if a big burden had been lifted from her.

"Betty," her mom said solemnly, "I know the pain that you are going through now, but I really do believe that you did the best thing. People—even a best friend or family—can be obstacles. Don't let people like that stop you from reaching your goal. You may feel alone at times, but in such situations you can draw from your inner strength to make it through. I know that this won't be easy, but be assured that the people who really love and care about you will be there to support you and help you accomplish your best."

"I know that you are right, Mom," said Betty in a sad voice. "But the pain—it's almost unbearable."

"You said it yourself," her mom said. "You used the words 'almost unbearable.' You see, the pain is not totally unbearable."

Betty looked at her mom with a gleam of hope in her eyes. "Mom," she said, "talking to you has made me feel better. You know what? I feel hungry. How about if I fix us both a snack? Then I really need to do my homework. I know that it's late but I've had a nap. Is it okay with you if I stay up for awhile to study after I do my homework?"

"Sure Betty. Try not to stay up too late," Betty's mom replied.

After they had their snack, Betty's mom went to bed while Betty finished her homework and studied her notes for a while. Then off she went to bed.

The following morning as Betty was leaving her house on her way to school, she saw Gabby standing under the big oak tree talking to Louise. As Betty approached her two friends, she addressed both of them; however, only Louise spoke back to her. Gabby turned her head away from Betty to avoid looking at her. For now, Gabby had made her choice.

While walking to school, Betty turned her thoughts back to her courses. She felt very good about school, for she understood all the material her teachers had given her so far. As the days went by, Betty began to experience a new feeling of confidence. She was sticking to her schedule and was doing very well in her courses. In fact, she received an *A* on her first calculus quiz. She maintained this standard of excellence, and at the end of the first semester, she made the honor roll—for the first time ever.

Time passed and Betty continued to do well in school. Her success had not gone unnoticed by Mr. Merman. One day, while getting ready to leave school, she heard someone behind her calling out her name. When she turned around, she saw Mr. Merman walking toward her.

"Betty," he said, "I would like to talk to you for a few minutes if you are not in a hurry."

"No, I am not in a hurry," said Betty. "Just let me put the books that I need to take home today in my book bag."

Mr. Merman and Betty silently walked back to his office. The silence was broken only after they entered his office. "Betty," he said, "I have something I would like to say to you. This is very difficult for me to do, but I believe that you deserve to hear this. I was wrong about you, Betty. I thought you were just like the others who made empty promises about doing better in school."

Mr. Merman became very reflective, "Looking back now, I realize that I was wrong for trying to discourage you, Maybe, just maybe, if I had encouraged other students and checked their progress... maybe some of them would have succeeded in their goals. When I first started this job 10 years ago, I was really excited about helping young people. Over the years though, my outlook has slowly changed, I have become disillusioned at what I have seen. However, your accomplishment is helping me to regain some of the hope and faith that I had when I first started this job."

"Thank you," said Betty. "Just hearing you say what you did makes me feel really good."

She picked up her book bag and walked toward the door. She turned around before opening the door and thanked Mr. Merman once again. She left his office and walked home. That day, another awakening had occurred-Mr. Merman's awakening to the untapped potential in others.

CHAPTER 3

Fight Betty, Fight!
Fight for What's Right!

Since Betty had became adjusted to her schedule and was doing well in school, she decided to begin an extracurricular activity. She had always had a love for cheerleading, so she decided to try out for the cheerleading squad. The tryouts were scheduled for the next day, so Betty hurried home from school to practice her routine.

Betty knew it was difficult to get on the squad. There were eight girls already on the squad and only two slots were open. She had heard through the school grapevine that 10 girls had signed up to try out. She decided to add several difficult flips to her cheer in order to help her beat the competition. She had always been very limber, so the flips were not difficult for her.

Betty stood looking at herself in the mirror, practicing until she was satisfied with her routine. "It would really be nice," Betty thought, "to have someone that could give me input on my routine. Mom doesn't get home from work until late and Gabby—well, that's another story. Uh . . .what I really need to do is to socialize with more people. Yes, I was hurt by what happened with Gabby, but that shouldn't stop me from making other friends."

Betty stayed up until she heard her mother opening the door downstairs. She hastened to tell her mother about everything that had happened to her that day. Her mom was excited about Betty's decision to try cheerleading. Her mom also wished, however, that she did not have to work such long hours. That way she could be at home when Betty arrived home from school every day.

"I feel that I'm missing out on so much," Betty's mom mused, "and I hate that you have to spend so much time alone. I have to keep this job though, at least for the time being."

Betty and her mom sat in deep silence for a while. Finally, her mom broke the silence. "Sometimes I wish that your father were here to see you, Betty," she said. "I know that he would be as proud of you as I am. Even though we never married, he loved you. He tried hard to succeed so that all of us could have a better life. To think that he died in a car accident when you were only five months old, never having seen you grow up to be an intelligent, beautiful young lady really saddens me."

"Mom," Betty responded. "Mom, I know I don't have any memories of my father since he died when I was so young, but I thank you for keeping him alive by telling me about him. I know through you, that he was a strong man who loved us both."

Betty tried to reassure her mom that she was doing an extraordinary job as a single parent. "Mom," she said, "I know that you are doing all you can for me. You give me plenty of love and encouragement. Without your support, I really don't know what I'd do."

Her mom responded with all the sensitivity she could muster. "I understand how you feel," she told Betty. "I know it's difficult for you to be without your father. It's like a part of you is missing. However, we have been making it and we will continue to make it. We may not have everything that we need or want, but we are making it."

Betty and her mom provided strong support for each other. That night, before they retired to bed, they expressed their gratitude to each other. "Thanks for being there for me, Mom," Betty said, hugging her mom.

"Thanks for being there for me, Betty," her mom responded. "Good night."

After school the next day, Betty hurriedly put on her bodysuit and tights. She wanted to practice one more time before the tryouts. She was in the gym practicing when two other girls who were trying out approached her. The one with the long, permed black hair introduced herself.

"Hi," she said. "My name is Laurie. My friend here is Mary." Like Laurie, Mary had long, permed black hair. Their skin was "honey-colored."

"We are both trying out for the squad," said Laurie as she ran her hand swiftly through her hair. "Have you heard that 10 girls are trying out this year and they only need two?"

Laurie wanted to intimidate Betty and possibly squash her intention to compete. With a smug expression on her face, Laurie declared, "From the looks of everyone else, I do believe that Mary and I have it made. Well, we have to go now and put on our bodysuits and tights."

Betty stood there very confused. She really didn't know what Laurie meant by saying that she and Mary "had it made" even before the tryouts began.

"Oh well," she thought to herself, "I can't become bogged down with that now." Soon it was time for the tryouts to begin. Mrs. Biggs and Mr. Kant were the judges.

"Girls," Mr. Kant said, "you're allowed to do a 10-minute routine. I'm asking each of you to be quiet while someone is performing."

All was quiet in the gym. The big moment had finally arrived for each girl to demonstrate her cheerleading skills. Mr. Kant glanced at all 10 contestants, then continued, "You will be judged on three things: one, your ability to cheer loudly and clearly; two, your ability to do difficult stunts; and three, your enthusiasm. I am assigning each of you a number from one to 10. When I call your number, I want you to walk down to the red circle in the middle of the gym. There, I want you to introduce yourself and tell us the name of the cheer that you will be doing. After the last person has finished, please don't come and ask me or Mrs. Biggs whether you have made the squad. The principal will announce on the intercom in the morning the two girls that we selected. Are there any questions?"

Betty stood up instantly to pose a question. "Mr. Kant," she said, "you mentioned that we will be judged on three areas. What is the maximum number of points that each of us can achieve in each of these areas?"

Mr. Kant responded briefly, "The maximum number of points you can receive in each area is 30. Are there any more questions?" After looking around the room to see if anyone else had a question, he said, "Good luck to each of you."

Mrs. Biggs began to pass out the assigned numbers. Betty's number was one. She liked being the first one, for she could get her performance over with, then relax and look at everyone else's routine.

Before long, Betty's number was called. She walked to the red circle in the middle of the floor and said in a clear, resounding voice, "Hello, my name is Betty Tate. The cheer that I am going to do is called *Take It To The Limit.*"

Ready! Okay!

Take it to the limit. Take it to the top.

We are the mighty Tigers and we can't be stopped.

Hey! Hey! What do you say?

Take that ball the other way.

Push them back. Push them back, way back.

Touchdown. That's what we want.

Touchdown.

After she finished her performance, Betty felt very good. She had done her entire routine without making any mistakes. Now she could relax and watch the other girls. Soon number two was called. Number two was Laurie. She seemed nervous—so nervous, in fact, that she fumbled over some words during the introduction and cheer. She did only one stunt, a half split.

"Wow," Betty thought, "I know that Laurie didn't make the squad. Anyone can do the half split. A whole split is the most difficult thing to do. Besides that, she did pretty bad on her cheer."

Laurie, however, did not seem to be the least bit upset over her performance. Instead of waiting and watching the rest of the girls, she went to the dressing room, put on her clothes, then left the gym. As she walked away, she had a smug look on her face.

Since Betty stayed behind to watch the other contestants perform, she had a fairly good idea of how she did in relation to the others; she was positive she had made the squad. She also believed that another girl named Betha had made it, for her routine was a rather difficult one, excellently performed.

After Betty changed into her school clothes, she walked over to Betha, who was putting her tights in her book bag.

"Hi," she said, smiling at Betha. "My name is Betty. I just want to tell you that your routine was very good. I believe that you will be one of the girls selected."

Betha laughed as she said resignedly, "You know what? This is my third year trying out for the squad, but I don't think I quite fit the image of the girls that they want on the squad. I'm laughing now—not because the situation is funny, but out of frustration. It sure beats crying. You were very good too, but I don't think that you fit their image either. . .Sometimes I wonder why I keep trying."

"I don't understand," Betty responded with a puzzled look on her face. "What do you mean by saying that we don't fit their image?"

"Have you ever taken a good long look at all the girls that are already on the squad?" Betha asked Betty. "Now take a look at yourself. Then you will see exactly what I mean."

Betty thought about the numerous times she had attended basketball and football games. On reflection, she could now recall that even though all of the cheerleaders were black, they were all light skinned with long hair. "No! No!" Betty thought as she tried to fool herself, "This must all be a coincidence."

In utter disbelief, Betty exclaimed to Betha, "No, I don't believe your conclusion regarding this situation. There must be some other reason. I'm pretty sure that it's all a coincidence."

"Well, think what you like," said Betha. "I too was like you at first, disbelieving the obvious. Sometimes neither talent nor knowledge matters. It's how you look. Well, I have to go home now. See you later."

After Betha left, Betty sat down on the bench by the locker staring at the wall. She thought about Laurie's boast that she and Mary had already made the squad. "It can't be true," she kept saying over and over to herself. Finally, she got up to leave for home. That night Betty had a difficult time trying to sleep. She tossed and turned for what appeared to be the entire night.

Finally, morning came. Betty could hardly wait to get to school, for this was the morning that the announcement would be made about which two girls had made the cheerleading squad. She quickly ate her breakfast and rushed off to school. Then she dashed off to her homeroom and sat eagerly waiting for the announcements to be made by the principal on the intercom.

One by one, the principal made the announcements. Soon she heard him say, "It is my privilege to announce the two new cheerleaders for the squad. They are Laurie Neal and Mary Watts."

Betty sat there in disbelief. She wondered how Laurie and Mary could have made the squad. Laurie had fumbled over some of her words and had done only one simple stunt. Mary had done okay, but several girls outdid her performance by far.

"How could this happen?" Betty wondered. Suddenly, she felt very ill. She quickly picked up her books and started walking out the door. As she hastened her steps out the door, she heard her teacher calling out her name, but Betty kept on walking. Once she got outside the school building, she started to run. She ran and ran until she was totally exhausted. Soon she had to stop to catch her breath, so she sat on a nearby park bench. "I need to talk to someone," Betty thought. "Mom didn't have to go to work today, so she should still be home. I'll go home and talk to my mom."

In spite of her exhaustion, she was so eager to get home that she sprang to her feet and ran all the way home. She was so tired that she leaned up against the doorbell after she pressed it, hoping that her mom would answer the door quickly. After a few minutes of pressing the doorbell, she sat down on the porch to search for her key in her book bag. She found the key, but in her exhaustion, she fumbled and it fell back down into her book bag.

The tears began to flow. Her entire body began to shake. She felt totally drained. Somehow she managed to get the key from her book bag and open the door. She dragged herself into the house and laid on the bare floor crying and beating the floor with her fists.

Finally, Betty reached the point where she felt that she could no longer cry. She got up and walked slowly into the bathroom to look at herself in the mirror. Her reflection showed a girl with a very dark complexion and medium-length hair parted all the way down the center and styled in two ponytails. She had brown eyes which were now red and swollen from crying. "Why?" she cried as she stared at her reflection. "What's the use of working hard for a goal if I will not be judged on my abilities? People are always saying that if you work hard, you can achieve your goals. Everyone makes it sound so easy. No one really stresses the external factors such as looks that can affect your life. Why?"

At this point, she was sobbing so hard that she didn't hear her mom come in from running errands. "Betty, Betty, what's wrong," her mom cried in great consternation. Betty was so overcome by tears that she could hardly speak. She looked at her mom and between sobs, she barely managed to tell her everything that had happened. Betty's mom reached out and took her in her arms and held her until she stopped crying.

Afterwards, Betty went into the bathroom to wash her face. While she was in the bathroom, her mom felt deep anguish over what Betty related to her.

"I must deal with my anger in a positive way," she thought, "so I can teach Betty that it's okay to be angry but to direct her anger positively."

When Betty came from the bathroom, her mom asked her to sit at the kitchen table. She fixed Betty a cup of hot chocolate. While Betty was drinking it, her mom called the school to let them know that Betty would not be returning that day to attend class. By the time she finished making the call, Betty was almost finished drinking her hot chocolate.

Betty's mom moved closer to the table so she could sit next to her daughter. "Betty," she said looking at her, "I too feel the anguish and the pain that you feel, for you are my child. It is sad to believe that there is prejudice within our race as well as outside our race; but Betty, this is reality. Neither you nor I can stop people from holding certain beliefs, but when their action infringes on our lives, then it's time to take action."

Betty's mom knew what action she wanted to take, but she wanted Betty to take an active role in the outcome of this crisis. Turning to her daughter, she said, "I need to know if you want to do anything about the situation. Before you answer though, I want you to know, just in case you say yes, that this could be a long, drawn-out battle. If you say no, then this would be the end of it for you. But for the other girls who 'don't fit the image,' this would be the beginning of their anguish and pain. Betty, it's your choice. Whatever your decision is, make sure that it's one you can live with."

Betty was torn between the need to vent her agony and indignation, and the need to take constructive action.

"Mom," Betty said in a pained voice, "what happened to me wasn't fair. I've cried so much that I now feel completely drained. What can we do, Mom? What can we do?"

"Good," her mom responded quickly, "I was hoping that you would want to find constructive ways to combat this problem. Let's both try to come up with solutions."

Betty's mom was a no-nonsense woman who knew how to get results. "Okay," she said in a take charge tone of voice. "First, I believe that we need to go and talk to Mrs. Biggs and Mr. Kant. If we don't get the results that we desire from them, then we will talk to the assistant principal and move up the chain of command."

"Okay," said Betty, "it's still early and I know that Mrs. Biggs and Mr. Kant have a free period in about 15 minutes. Could you call and see if they can talk to us on such short notice?"

"No, Betty, I won't call," said her mom, "I believe that you should do it. I'll help you all I can, but you also have to help yourself. I want you to call the school and once you make the appointment, I want you to talk to them."

"But Mom. . .," Betty protested.

"No, you have to do this for yourself," her mom retorted in a gentle but firm voice.

Betty reluctantly picked up the phone and called the school. After talking to Mrs. Biggs for a few minutes, she hung up the phone and told her mom that they could go to the school right away. Betty went to the bathroom to double check her face before going back to school. Her eyes were still red and somewhat swollen from crying. To camouflage this, she quickly dashed some cold water on her face. "Hopefully," she thought, "no one will notice it."

Off they went to school. When they arrived at the school, Mrs. Biggs and Mr. Kant were waiting in the office for them in order to direct them to the meeting room. Once they were all seated, Mrs. Biggs commented, "From the conversation that I had with you, Betty, I understand that you are disappointed that you didn't make the squad. We are sorry but there is nothing that we can do about it. We have made our choice and it is final."

Betty was undaunted by Mrs. Biggs' inflexible response. In a calm, collected voice, she reminded Mrs. Biggs about the criteria for judging the routine.

"Prior to the tryouts," Betty said, looking directly at Mrs. Biggs, "you said that each of us would be judged in three categories: enthusiasm, ability to cheer loudly and difficult stunts. How then, can you explain Laurie making the squad when she stumbled over words during her introduction and during her cheer? Furthermore, she did only one simple stunt. Also, can you explain to us why all the girls on the squad have long hair and a light complexion?"

"Well. . .uh. . .you see. . .uh," mumbled Mrs. Biggs, "I really don't have to explain myself to you. Some things cannot be changed and this is one of them, so leave it alone." She then stood up to indicate that, as far as she was concerned, their meeting was over.

"Well, Mrs. Biggs," said Betty's mom in an indignant but controlled voice, "as far as you are concerned, it may be over with. But for Betty and I, this is just the beginning. You are right in saying that some things can't be changed. The color of Betty's skin and the texture of her hair cannot be changed naturally. But you know what? We can sure try to change the system. We'll start by going now to talk to the assistant principal, Mr. King." At that point, Betty and her mom stood up to leave.

"Wait a minute," cried Mr. Kant. "This incident has been blown out of perspective. I'm sure that we can work something out. There is really no need for you to talk to the assistant principal. How about if we make you an alternate cheerleader? If one of the other cheerleaders can't make a game, then you can take her place."

Betty laughed at this attempted compromise. "Do you think you can pull the wool over my eyes by offering to make me an alternate cheerleader?" she said mockingly. "Well, you are wrong about me. I don't want your alternate position. I only want what I deserve. You make it seem as if you are doing me a favor by giving me something. Well, you're not. Thanks, but no thanks, for your offer."

Betty and her mom left the office, ignoring Mr. Kant's pleas for them to "just be reasonable." When they arrived at Mr. King's office, he was preparing to leave. Realizing that Mr. King was on his way out, Betty's mom addressed him. "Mr. King," she began, "my name is Miss Tate and I am Betty's mom. I know that we don't have an appointment with you, but this is an urgent matter."

Mr. King obliged. "I was just going to lunch," he said, "but you've convinced me that this is an important matter, so please come into my office and have a seat." Once she was seated, Betty quickly proceeded to explain the reason for their unplanned office visit.

Mr. King was unmoved by Betty's explanation and petition. "This matter is really out of my hands," Mr. King stated quite deliberately. "I know Mrs. Biggs and Mr. Kant, and I can personally say that they are both excellent teachers."

"I am not questioning their ability to teach," said Betty, "but I am questioning their judgement on the selection of the two cheerleaders. If you choose to overlook this matter, then we will go to the principal and whoever else we need to see."

"I see," Mr. King said in a conciliatory voice. "All right, but first I need to talk to Mrs. Biggs and Mr. Kant. I will call you this evening after I've talked with them. I'm sure that we can come up with some practical solutions."

"That's fine," said Betty, as she and her mom got up from their chairs to leave.

As soon as they arrived home, Betty's mom received a call from Mrs. Bell asking her if she minded coming to work, even though it was her off day. Betty's mom needed the extra money, so soon she was out the door again—this time headed for work. After she left, Betty got out her books to study, but she was so preoccupied with the day's events that she found it difficult to concentrate on her studies.

"I know what I can do," Betty thought. "I can call Betha, but I don't know where she lives. . .I know what I can do. I will call all the Wrights in the telephone book and ask if a Betha lives there." She got out the telephone book and looked under "Wright". Fortunately, there were only 10 Wrights listed. The first three calls were unsuccessful. However on the fourth call, Betty recognized Betha's voice as she answered the phone.

"Betha," Betty began, "this is Betty Tate. Remember, I am the one that you talked to after the cheerleading tryouts. As you found out in school today, neither one of us made the squad. You were at the tryouts yourself and you saw all the mistakes that Laurie made, yet she was still selected. Mary was fine, but several other girls did better than she."

"Yes, I remember talking to you," Betha replied, "Now you see that what I told you happened to be true." Betha became reflective and somewhat philosophical. "You know, life goes on," she continued. "You just have to deal with it the best way that you can. I really didn't expect to make it anyway, but I must say I still had a spark of hope."

"No! No! No!" Betty cried, almost yelling. "Neither one of us has to just deal with the situation on our own. It's not our problem, but the problem is being placed on us. The problem is really within other people—within their system of thinking."

Betty then explained to Betha what had happened at school that day. "The assistant principal is supposed to be calling me this evening," Betty said. "If he decides to do nothing about the situation, I would like you to go with me tomorrow to talk to the principal."

"No, oh no," protested Betha, "I couldn't do that. You see, I really don't want to start any trouble. You should leave this alone; otherwise, you may end up in more trouble than you can imagine. I learned early in life not to rock the boat, as some would say. You really should think about this, too."

"No," Betty said with determination in her voice, "I don't have to think about it anymore. Sometimes Betha, you have to fight for what you believe in. You need to think about what you are really losing by being passive. If our ancestors had remained passive, we wouldn't have made any progress. My mind is definitely made up. I see that you have made up your mind, too, though. But if you change your mind, please let me know. I have to go now because I don't want to tie up the phone line."

After Betty hung up the phone, she felt somewhat disappointed. No, she wasn't angry with Betha.

In fact, she understood why Betha responded the way she did. She knew that she was an excellent student who was trying to win a scholarship to college. To do this, she needed the recommendations of some of her teachers. She really didn't know how her teachers would react if she accused Mrs. Biggs and Mr. Kant of favoritism. Understandably, she did not want to risk taking that chance.

Just then the phone rang. It was Mr. King. "Betty," he said in a conciliatory voice, "I talked to Mrs. Biggs and Mr. Kant. They denied your charges against them. This is a very serious charge that could lead to strife in the school. To prevent this, I told Mrs. Biggs and Mr. Kant that we will have a new tryout for the cheerleaders. This time, though, Mrs. Biggs and Mr. Kant will not be the judges. I have selected two people who I believe to be unbiased. These two people are from the community. The tryout is tomorrow after school. You will be judged on the same three areas as before. I can't promise you that you will make the squad, but if you are as good as you say you are, I'm sure that you will. Well, I have to go now, for I have to call the other girls."

Betty was very excited after she hung up the phone. "Let me go ahead and do my homework," she thought, "and then I can practice some more on my routine." After doing her homework and putting in some study time, Betty went before the mirror to practice her routine. Just then, she heard her mom's key in the door.

"Hi, Mom," Betty cried excitedly, "I have some really great news!" She began to tell her mom everything that had happened. Naturally, her mom was just as excited as she was. In fact, they got so carried away in their excitement that they ended up talking for about an hour, before they both went upstairs to prepare themselves for the next day.

Betty woke up a little earlier than usual the next morning. She got dressed quickly and then ran downstairs. Since Betty was the first one to go downstairs, she proceeded to prepare breakfast for herself and her mom. However, at breakfast that morning, she said very little to her mom, as her thoughts were fixed on the repeat tryout later in the day.

At school that morning, she saw Betha waiting for her next to her locker. "Betty," said Betha with some eagerness in her voice, "Mr. King called me and told me about everyone trying out for cheerleading again today. Ever since I got the call last night, I have been thinking about the conversation that we had on the phone. Betty, I know that I was wrong, but you have to understand that I am scared. You see, I am working hard in school to try to win a scholarship to college. My parents can't afford to send me. No one else in my family has even completed high school, so for me to go to college is like a dream. My family is depending on me Betty, and I can't risk ruining my chances. I just don't need any added pressure in my life right now."

"Betha," Betty cried in a compassionate tone, "I'm not angry at you. I really do understand why you did what you did. You did what you felt you had to do. The most important thing is that you faced up to the situation, instead of denying it."

"Thank you for at least understanding," said Betha with tears in her eyes.

The bell rang and they both rushed off to their class. The school day passed slowly for Betty, but finally the last bell rang to dismiss school for the day. Betty went to the gym and changed into her bodysuit and tights. Then she went to have a seat on the bleachers and waited for the tryouts to begin. She saw that all of the cheerleaders who had tried out the last time were now in the gym. The two judges were now coming into the gym with Mr. King.

Mr. King walked up to the microphone and addressed those present. "I have already informed each of you why you have to try out for the squad again," he began. "You will be judged on the same three areas as before. The maximum score you can receive in each area is 30, with the highest maximum score in all three areas being 90. After the final scores are tallied, you are all welcome to come up and look at them." Mr. King then introduced the judges. Finally, he told them that the two cheerleaders would be announced in the gym about 15 minutes after the tryouts.

The tryouts went basically like the first one. Once again Betty felt very confident that she, along with Betha, had made it. Afterwards all the girls went to the dressing room to put on their regular clothes. While Betty was dressing, Laurie came up to her and angrily said, "You had no right Betty to do this! You are just jealous of me. Yes, I realize that my cheer and stunt were not nearly as good as yours or any of the other girls. But you know what? I am prettier than you and the others. You probably have always had to work hard for what you want. But me, well, my looks will get me what I want in life. I definitely got what it takes and you—well, look in the mirror at yourself!" Then she angrily walked away.

At that moment, Betha came into the dressing room and announced that the judges had made their decision. Betty quickly went into the gym with the others to wait. There, Mr. King was standing, waiting to make the announcement. "Each of you did a good job," he began, "but two of the girls did a superb job." He paused for a moment. "I am pleased to announce the names of the two new cheerleaders: Betty Tate and Betha Wright."

Betha ran over to Betty and gave her a big hug. Immediately, Laurie got up and angrily stomped out of the gym. But all of the other girls went over to congratulate Betty and Betha.

"I am really glad that you two made the squad," Mary said, as she congratulated Betty and Betha. "Laurie and I really didn't deserve to make it. We both knew why we were chosen, but we went right along with it. We were wrong, though. Laurie is angry, but I'm not. I believe you both earned this honor, so it is rightfully yours."

"Thank you. Thank you," said Betty and Betha appreciatively. That day more than one awakening had occurred—an awakening that could promote growth or destroy human lives.

CHAPTER 4

From Girlhood to Womanhood

Time passed and Betty enjoyed being a cheer leader. She was still keeping up with her studies and making the honor roll. Now, at age 16, she could look back and laugh to herself when she thought about how she was determined at age 15 to drop out of school and work. To even think that she was eager to drop out of school seemed stupid to her now. "Well," she thought, "life involves growth and making choices. At least I am making the right choices now."

Now she was really enjoying her school activities. Her mind had completely changed from what it was when she was 15. At that time, she believed she had all the answers.

What was even more interesting in her life was that Dan, a football player, had asked her to go out with him to their junior class dance. She told him that she would let him know after talking it over with her mom. That afternoon, Betty practically ran home from school, hoping that she would arrive home before her mom left for work. By the time she got home though, her mom had already left.

Betty was really excited. She knew that her mom would let her go to the dance because she had already said Betty could start dating at age 16.

Up until now though, she had never really been interested in dating. Yes, she noticed boys and even thought some of them were cute, but she could never picture herself going out with a boy. She would sometimes hear girls laughing and talking in the gym room about boys, but she never joined in. Most of the girls she knew had started dating earlier than the age of 16. Most of those girls were into fancy hairstyles, makeup, and the latest fashions.

Well, Betty was still wearing her hair parted down the middle and styled in two ponytails. She had never tried applying make-up and never bothered with all the fashionable styles. She knew that her mom couldn't afford all the latest fashionable styles.

"But," she thought, "I can experiment with a little make-up. It is not that expensive. Also, I can experiment with different styles. Let me see now. I know what I can do. Mom used to wear make-up. Maybe she's still got some around."

Betty looked in her mother's jewelry box, which was really an old cigar box with manila paper covering the outside. There Betty found a tube of lipstick and some eye shadow.

"Well," she thought, "this is better than nothing. I can experiment with this at least."

When she opened up the lipstick, she found that it was a dark shade of brown. Eagerly, she applied it to her lips. And even though she was not a trained expert, she thought that the color looked really pretty on her. Next, she opened the eye shadow, which was a lighter shade of brown than the lipstick. After applying it, she looked at herself in the mirror and was quite pleased with the overall effect.

"Okay," she thought, "now I need to do something about my hair." She took down both of her ponytails and combed all of her hair back from her face.

"Maybe I could wear my hair in one ponytail to the side," she thought. "Then again, I need a more sophisticated style. I know what I can do. I can use mom's old hair rollers. Then I can try styling it once it is curled. If I roll it up now, it should be curled by the time mom gets home."

After she rolled up her hair, Betty ate dinner and started to study. By the time she finished studying, her mom arrived home.

"Wow," her mom teased. "What do we have here? I see that my little girl is growing up."

"Mom, guess what?" cried Betty, "A boy named Dan on the football team invited me to go to the junior class school dance! I told him I would talk to you about it first."

"Betty," her mom said, "I think this is great. But first tell me what do you know about Dan. Also, I would really like to meet him before he takes you out."

"I really don't know too much about him except that he is on the football team. I have seen him around school many times, though. I know what I can do. How about if I invite him over to the house? Then you can learn more about him. But please, Mom, don't ask him too many questions."

Laughing, her mom said, "Betty, I can remember telling my mom the same thing. But don't worry, I won't ask him too many questions. I definitely want

to check him out though, before he takes you any-
where. Yes, I know you have pretty good judgment,
but I would feel more comfortable knowing more
about him."

"That's fine, Mom. But I just don't want him to
feel as if he's on trial," said Betty.

"Like I said, don't worry about it. I know how to
ask the right questions. Mrs. Bell gave me the day
off tomorrow, for she's going out of town. How about
asking him to come over after school?"

Betty went over to the phone and called Dan to
see if he could come over after school the next day.
After checking with his parents, he told her that he
could. Betty was excited as well as a little scared.
This would be the first time she had ever entertained
a boy at her house.

"Well," she thought, "let me get up and see how
my hair looks. I want everything to be just perfect."

Betty's mom took the rollers from Betty's hair for
her. Betty was quite surprised at the difference a
new hairstyle and a little make-up made in her ap-
pearance. She felt like a different person. As she
looked at herself in the mirror, she no longer saw a
girl with two ponytails on each side, but a girl blos-
soming, growing into womanhood. That day another
awakening occurred—an awakening that every girl
experiences when she passes from girlhood to
womanhood.

CHAPTER 5

Stepping Out

The next morning, Betty woke up early so she could do some work around the house. Dan was coming over and she wanted to have everything just right for him. First, she went downstairs to the living room. In the living room was an old brown couch. Its springs were so worn that it practically sunk to the floor. The rest of the furniture was just as worn as the couch. But even though all of the furniture was very worn, Betty and her mom had always taken great care to keep the room clean. You see, Betty's mom had always taught her that no matter how much or little you have, you should take care of it.

However at this point, Betty felt depressed looking at the room. She couldn't help but think about the nice furniture that Mrs. Bell had. In comparison, their furniture looked like a pile of junk.

"I know what I can do," Betty thought. "I can pick some flowers and put them on the table."

She went walking to look for pretty flowers. After she returned home, she put the flowers into some water in the vase she found in the attic.

"Wow," she thought. "The flowers are really pretty.

They definitely brighten up the room. Well, it's time for me to go to school now, so I better hurry."

Betty got her book bag and off she went to school. When she got to school, she saw Dan getting out of a red sports car. The car looked new to Betty. She wondered whose car he was in. "Could this be his car?" she wondered. "If so, how could he afford it? No, it can't be his car," she concluded to herself.

Betty had noticed before that Dan was always very neatly dressed. She could tell by looking at his clothes that they were expensive. Now to see him in a red sports car was quite overwhelming. "Could his family be very well off financially?" she wondered. "I'm pretty sure he can see that I'm poor. I shouldn't think the worst. Maybe he's sincerely interested in me. Time will tell."

Betty noticed that Dan was now walking towards her. "Betty," he said with a gleam in his eyes, "how are you doing this morning? You are still expecting me over after school today, aren't you?"

"I'm doing fine," she answered calmly, trying to disguise her excitement, "and yes, I am still expecting you after school today. My mom is really looking forward to meeting you."

"Great," said Dan, as he was about to walk away. "And by the way, I like your new hairstyle."

"He noticed," said Betty to herself, "and he actually likes it. He really did notice my hair!"

For the remainder of the day, Betty felt as if she were walking on air. She practically ran home after school to make sure that everything was still the way she wanted it to be. When she opened the door, the house smelled really good. "What is that good smell?" she wondered. She walked into the kitchen and saw that her mom was taking out her last batch of cookies from the oven. On the table her mom had a pitcher of milk and some of her freshly baked cookies on a platter.

"Mom," Betty said, "it smells so good in here. What kind of cookies did you bake?"

She picked up one from the platter and took a bite. "Um, um, this really tastes good. Cinnamon cookies are my favorite too," Betty said. "Thank you for everything you have done to help make this special for me, Mom. We may not have all the money that we need, but I consider myself rich by having a mother like you. Thanks for everything."

She took her book bag to her bedroom. Then she went to the bathroom to check her hair and wash up. She heard the doorbell ring while she was in the bathroom. Instead of hurrying down, she decided to stay in the bathroom longer than really necessary to give her mom time alone with Dan. When Betty came out the bathroom, she heard her mom and Dan talking and laughing. She walked on down the stairs to greet Dan.

"Hi, Dan," she said in a chirpy voice. "I see that you and my mom are getting along fine."

"Yes, we are," he said. "I was nervous about meeting your mom at first, but she really has put me at ease. I'm really glad that I came."

"I'm glad too that you did come," her mom said reassuringly. "I just wanted to meet you before you took my daughter out, and I like what I see, too."

They all laughed and the afternoon proceeded very well. Betty found out some of the answers to her questions about Dan. She found out that he lived in the suburbs and that his father was a mechanical engineer and his mom was a college professor. The kids from his neighborhood were bused to the inner city area to attend school. Dan's parents could have put him in a private school to avoid this, but they decided to let him attend public school for a while because Dan wanted a change. He discovered that he really liked that school, primarily because the teachers were good. For him, this compensated for the fact that this school had less modern equipment than his former school.

Soon it was time for Dan to leave. As Betty walked him to the door, she saw the red sports car by the curb.

"Dan," said Betty, "I saw you in a red sports car at school today, and now I see that same car by the curb. Is it your car?"

"Yes," answered Dan, "my parents brought it for me on my sixteenth birthday so I wouldn't have to ride the bus to school."

"It is very nice," said Betty. "I love the color. In fact, red is my favorite color."

"Thank you," replied Dan. "Now we need to talk about the dance tomorrow night. It starts at eight o'clock, so is it okay if I pick you up about seven fifteen?"

"Yes, that's fine with me," she said.

"Well, I will see you tomorrow then," he said as he walked down the steps.

When Dan left, Betty ran back in the house. She was so happy. Everything was really working out great for her. She was going to attend her first dance tomorrow night.

"The dance!" cried Betty. "Mom, I don't have any-
thing to wear. I have been so excited about going to
the dance that I forgot that I have absolutely noth-
ing to wear to it."

"You may have forgotten about it, but I didn't,"
said her mom. "While you were at school today, I
went to the store and brought some material. In fact,
I brought your favorite color. Tell me what style dress
you want and I will make it for you right now."

Betty had almost forgotten that her mom could
sew. It had been so long since she had actually seen
her mom sew anything. While her mom went to get
the sewing machine out of the closet, Betty decided
to sketch a picture of the gown she wanted. She felt
really fortunate because her mom could sew with-
out a pattern. She could simply look at the picture
of any outfit, then make it.

When Betty finished sketching the picture, her
mom sat down at the sewing machine and began to
make her dress. Within a couple of hours, her mom
finished sewing the dress. Betty just stood there look-
ing while her mom held the dress up so that she
could see. To Betty, the dress was so beautiful that
she could hardly wait until it was time to go to the
dance. That night as she slept, she could visualize
herself dancing in her red dress, swirling round and
round. The following night, her dream would become
a reality for her.

The night of the dance finally arrived. Betty put
on her dress while her mom waited to zip up the
back for her. When she was finally ready, she danced
around the room in anticipation of the dance.

Finally, the doorbell rang. Betty ran to take one
last look at herself in the mirror while her mom an-

swered the door. When Betty entered the living room and saw Dan, she felt that her heart was pounding so loud that she imagined her mom and Dan heard it, too. "Wow!" she thought, "He looks really good." Dan had on a black suit with a gray shirt and a black and gray striped tie. In his hand was a small box. He handed the box to Betty.

"What's this?" she nervously asked while removing the bow.

"This is a corsage that I brought for you. I forgot to ask you what color your dress would be, so I brought white because it would blend in with any other color. May I pin it on for you Betty?" asked Dan.

"Thank you," said Betty. "It's very nice. You can pin it on my right shoulder for me."

After saying their good-byes to Betty's mom, they left for the dance. At the car, Dan opened Betty's door for her. He then slid into the driver's seat and off they went. It was a very beautiful evening, so Dan decided to roll down the top of his convertible. The wind was gently blowing and the moon was a glimmering yellow.

"This is really great," Betty thought. It was her first time ever riding in a sports car. She was having a good time just riding in the car with Dan.

When they arrived at the dance, she could see people staring at them and whispering. This was her first time ever to attend a dance, so everyone was surprised to see her. To top it off, she was with Dan, who was well known in school, not only as a top football player, but as a honor student and leader in many school organizations.

"Oh well," she thought, "I'm planning on having a good time tonight, so they can whisper all that they want to."

At the dance, Betty found out that Dan loved to dance just as much as she did. They danced to nearly every record. During intermission, Betty went to the powder room to freshen up. Inside were Laurie and a group of other girls that Betty knew vaguely from school. Laurie stopped talking to the other girls when Betty walked in. She stood and stared at Betty angrily while Betty stood by the mirror freshening up her make-up. When she was about to leave, Laurie walked in front of the door, blocking the way out.

"Well, hello there," sneered Laurie. "You must think that you are hot stuff. You took away my position on the squad and now you think that you are going to take Dan away from me. Honey, you and he are definitely not in the same class! Like I told you before, take a good long look at yourself. You may be smart but you have absolutely nothing else going for you. Look at you in your cheap red dress. Where did you find it? At the dump? You just remember that I had Dan first and I will get him back."

"Get out of my way," said Betty.

"Sure," laughed Laurie. "Remember that you have Dan for now, but I will get him back."

Betty hurried out of the powder room. Once she was back inside the dance room, she went over to Dan who was standing by the punch bowl.

"I'm back," she said.

"I see. Uh, is everything okay?" said Dan. "You look upset."

"No, I'm fine," said Betty, "I am not going to let Laurie ruin my evening."

"Laurie," he cried. "What does she have to do with this?"

"Let's just enjoy our evening and we can talk about it later. I'm really doing fine," said Betty.

"Fine. We can talk about it later on the way home. The music is playing again. Would you like to dance?"

"Sure," said Betty, and off they went to dance away the remainder of the evening. When the dance ended at eleven o'clock, they decided to leave right away, instead of hanging out with some of the other kids. Betty had a midnight curfew, so they decided that they should head back to her house so they wouldn't be late. They arrived back there about 40 minutes before the curfew ended.

"Betty," said Dan, "now I would like to hear about your encounter with Laurie. But first I want to tell you about my relationship with her. Well, we dated a couple of times. I just found out that she is really not my type. She's more into how good she looks and how much money her family has. She lives in the same neighborhood as I do. My parents know her parents very well. That is really all there is to our relationship—if you can call it that."

Betty then told Dan some of what Laurie had said. Before she could finish, he said, "That's enough, I really don't want to hear anymore. Betty, I like you a lot as a person. My parents taught me to look beyond a person's clothing and to look at the inner being. When I look at you, I see a person that I can respect. You are attractive and you are smart. I felt really proud to be with you tonight. I heard the whispering and saw people staring. Why? I don't know and I really don't care. I hope that you'll continue to go out with me. I'd like to spend more time with you."

This all seemed like a beautiful dream to Betty. The only difference was that this dream was a reality in her life. This was quite amazing to her. Before now, she never could have imagined this being real in her life. To her it was another awakening—that dreams can become reality.

CHAPTER 6

The Dinner Party

Time passed and Betty and Dan continued to date. After about three months of dating, Dan invited Betty to come to his house for dinner. His parents were very eager to meet her and Betty was really excited about meeting them. From what Dan had told her about them, she knew that they were very down-to-earth people. They both were poor when growing up, but had worked hard in order to attain the success they now enjoyed. "At least," she thought, "they will understand what I am trying to do." She really wanted to make a good impression on them. Dan, however, told her not to worry about it, for if he liked her, he was sure that his parents would also.

The day of the dinner finally arrived. Dan came to Betty's home to pick her up so she wouldn't have to catch the bus. As they approached Dan's house, Betty was surprised to discover that he lived in the same neighborhood as Mrs. Bell, the lady that her mom worked for. Once again, she saw the beautiful houses with the pretty flowers and shrubbery surrounding them. She remembered the first time that she saw these houses with her mother, and how she thought that she could see the inside of such homes only in magazines. Now to think that she was going inside one—not to work, but as a guest!

When they arrived at Dan's house, his mother and father, Mr. and Mrs. Allen, greeted Betty very warmly.

"Betty," said Mrs. Allen, "I'm really glad to finally meet you. Dan has told us so much about you."

"I'm really glad to meet both of you," replied Betty. "From listening to Dan talk about both of you, I know that he has a lot of admiration and respect for you."

"Well, you can go and wash up for dinner," said Mrs. Allen, "and then we can talk some more. I am really looking forward to getting to know you better."

While Betty and Dan were washing up, his mother and father eagerly waited for the young couple to join them in the dining room. When Betty walked into the dining room, she was awestruck. She thought it was the most beautiful room that she had ever seen. Over the dining table was a big chandelier. It was so resplendent that it reminded her of how droplets of rain glisten on leaves when the sun comes out brightly after a rain-drenched day. It was such a beautiful sight to see! On one wall was a large china cabinet that stretched from one side of the wall to the next. Inside were different kinds of dishes that Mr. Allen had brought overseas when he was in the Navy. Dan had told her all about the many years they spent living in several different countries overseas while his father was in the Navy.

"Betty," said Mr. Allen, playing the hospitable host, "come and sit down. We want to hear all about you. Dan has told us quite a bit about you, but of course, as parents, we want to know more. Tell me, what do your parents do for a living?"

"Wow," she thought to herself as she went to sit on the chair that Mr. Allen was pointing to. "I have a feeling that they're both going to ask me lots and lots of questions. Look at all this silverware on the table for just one meal! This is really quite unbelievable."

Betty told them all about her mom and dad. It seemed to her that the more she answered their questions, the more they asked her. She felt like she was on trial and that Mr. and Mrs. Allen were the jury. She was very surprised by all the questions; but then again, she felt they meant no harm. She felt that they were curious about the girl that their son was dating.

Regardless of their reason, Betty felt quite uncomfortable. Trying to figure out which piece of silverware to use with each dish was even more burdensome. So Betty decided to watch Mrs. Allen to see what piece of silverware she used. "To think," she thought, "that you are supposed to eat soup with a certain spoon rather than a regular spoon! A regular spoon would serve the same purpose!"

By the time dinner was over, Betty felt even more uneasy. She just wasn't sure if they liked her. Yes, they had asked her lots of seemingly innocent questions, but still she felt something just was not right. At times, when she was answering their questions, she would notice Mrs. Allen glancing at Mr. Allen. This was very puzzling to her. "Well, I'll just have to ask Dan what is going on when we are alone," thought Betty. Hopefully, he will know—even though he himself had a puzzled look on his face throughout the evening.

Soon the time came for Dan to take Betty back home. After saying goodbye to Dan's parents, Betty silently sighed in relief that the dinner was over. While they were walking to the car, she eagerly asked Dan, "What do you think your parents thought of me? They asked me so many questions that I felt uncomfortable."

"I was surprised by all the questions they asked you," answered Dan. "I really don't think my parents meant any harm, though. I think that they were just curious. Remember, I told you that my parents taught me never to judge a person by the exterior, but by the inner being. The main thing is that you are a good and loving person. My parents had to struggle to get to the point where they are today, so why should they look down on you?"

"Well, I guess you know your parents better than I. Even though what you said *should* make me feel much better, I actually don't. I don't know what it is, but something is not quite right."

They didn't say very much to each other the rest of the way to Betty's house. Betty was deep in thought over why Dan's parents asked so many questions. Even though Dan kept his doubts from Betty, he too was wondering why his parents asked her so many questions. He had never seen his parents act this way toward his dates before. This was definitely something different.

Dan started reflecting on his parents' attitude toward his dates. He recalled that the last girl he brought home was Laurie. He only did this because his parents kept urging him to have her over to the house. He knew that his parents really liked her, and that they had known her and her parents for many years. When he stopped dating her, they were perturbed and even tried to arrange a secret meeting to get them back together again. It didn't work, though. He saw through Laurie and had no interest in ever dating her again. He even told his parents this but they shrugged it off and urged him to give her another chance. They never did mention it again, so he thought they understood.

"Like I told Betty," he thought to himself, "the most important thing they taught me is that I should never judge a person by how much they possess, but by their inner being. My parents have always been true to their word, so I know that Betty is mistaken. I need to rid myself of my doubts, too."

When Betty returned to her house that evening, she told her mom everything that had happened. Her mom told her to try not to let it worry her, even though she knew that this would be difficult to do. Betty tried to take her advice, but she ended up tossing and turning nearly all night. The next morning, she woke up feeling tired because of her lack of sleep the night before. She took a long warm bath that helped her to relax somewhat. At least she felt a little less tense now.

After breakfast she headed to school. As soon as she arrived there, she saw Dan parking his car. She walked over to him.

"Hi," she said. "I see that you are arriving at school a little later than usual, too. In fact, the late bell should be ringing in about nine minutes."

"Yes, I am a little later than usual," he said. "I had something else to do before coming to school."

"Something is wrong with Dan," thought Betty. "He looks as if he didn't sleep well last night either.

Also, he's not giving me eye contact like he usually does. He just seems to be looking past me."

"Dan, is something wrong?" she asked with great concern in her voice.

"No, of course not," he answered quickly. "What could possibly be wrong? I just have to go now. I don't want to be late for homeroom."

"Dan," cried Betty as he walked away from her, "can we meet for lunch today or maybe talk after school?"

"No," stammered Dan. "I really can't today. I have other plans. I really have to go now. I. . .uh. . well. . .I will call you."

He quickly walked away and headed to his homeroom. Betty stood there for a few seconds thinking about what had just happened. Then she quickly walked to her homeroom so she wouldn't be late. By the time school ended for the day, she decided that she would try to talk to Dan again to find out what was going on. Just then, she saw him walking to his car, so she decided to run to catch up with him. Dan turned around and saw her running toward him, but he kept walking.

"Dan," cried Betty, "I really need to talk to you. Something is wrong and I would like to know what it is. I know that you are trying to avoid me, so could you please tell me the reason why. I know I can't make you tell me anything, but I just assumed that we had a relationship based on honesty. Was I wrong?"

Dan stopped walking and turned slowly around. "Betty," he nervously said, "I do owe you an explanation for my behavior. This is really difficult for me to say, but. . .well. . .uh. . .I really don't know the right way to say this, or even if there is a right way."

"Just come straight out and tell me what you have to say. Forget about trying to choose the right words, just say it, please," cried Betty.

"Okay," he said. "My parents liked you a lot as a person, but they don't feel that. . .well. . .that you don't have the proper upbringing that my girlfriend should have. Betty, they know that you are intelligent, but still. . .Betty, it is really just hard for me to explain."

Betty felt as if she was experiencing a horrible nightmare and needed to escape. She was so stunned that she could hardly get the words out of her mouth. "Dan," she said, "you told me that your parents didn't care how much or how little money a person possesses. You also told me that their emphasis has always been on the inner being."

"Well, that's true," he said. "But you see, I was brought up in a certain lifestyle—one that is very different from yours. You would have a lot to learn in order to fit into my lifestyle."

"Dan," she said, "you told me that your parents were very poor when they were growing up, so how can they look down on me now?"

"My parents are not looking down on you," he said angrily. "You just have to understand, Betty. Yes, my parents are from a poor background and they had a lot to learn in order to fit in their present status, but they were able to learn together. With us, I would have to teach you simple things such as which piece of silverware to use for a certain course. My parents really didn't give me a choice in this matter. They insisted that I break it off with you. They believe that it's best for both of us. My parents have always been there for me. With Laurie, I went against their wishes, but this time it's different. I can't ever recall seeing them so upset before. I really have to abide by what they think regardless of how right we seem to be for each other. We can still remain friends, though."

"So-o-o," Betty said sarcastically, "your parents don't think that I am good enough to be your girl-friend, huh? I am lacking in certain social skills according to them, huh? So they gave their little boy permission for us to be mere friends. Well, let me tell you something, Dan Allen. I would prefer not to have you as a friend. Who knows—if I did agree that we could be friends, I would never know when your parents may decide that I'm not worthy enough to be your friend. I'm pretty sure that I would be one friend that you would keep hidden from all your real friends. Forget it, okay? When I see you, I will speak to you—but that's it!"

Betty walked away, oblivious to Dan's cries for her to come back. She walked away to build a new life, one that would be without Dan. That day another awakening occurred for Betty. It was one that would test her strength to survive. Yes, it was a crushing experience, but one that she knew she would not allow to crush her completely. In her mind, she knew that she would survive.

CHAPTER 7

Facing the Past

Well, life went on for Betty. No, everything didn't fall in place exactly the way she wanted it to at all times, but she had learned not to let any situation totally crush her. Sure, she had gotten hurt in several situations, but it didn't stop her.

She knew that some kids at school took drugs and alcohol to help make them forget their hurts and pain.

Within herself, she knew that this wasn't the answer for her. Sure, many people are duped into thinking that substance abuse eases the pain. But in the long run, it exacts a terrible toll. Besides that, Betty wanted to be in control and not to be controlled by any substance. Yes, a lot of hard work was involved in staying clear of drugs and alcohol, but it was worth it to her. It took a lot of mental, as well as physical work to stay clear of substance abuse. Sure, it would have been much easier for her to feel sorry for herself and to give up. She didn't, though. Betty knew within herself that the only way she had out of the ghetto was to get an education. She had made her choice.

As she achieved more and more of her personal goals, she became more and more confident of herself. This boosted her to pursue more and more of her goals, no matter how discouraging the circumstances seemed. Now, as she neared the end of her senior year, she recalled that one of the goals she had set for herself was to be the valedictorian of her senior class. As the valedictorian, she would be the student speaker at her graduation.

What was rather unusual about her wanting to achieve this honor was that she didn't want it for the popularity associated with it. That was secondary to her. She wanted to be valedictorian because she believed she had a message to tell—one of faith and belief in yourself. In her neighborhood, there were many who were strung out on drugs and alcohol. Some had simply given up on life and had became complacent. Betty truly believed that if she could make it, anyone could. "If my message only helped one person," Betty thought, "it would definitely be worthwhile."

Soon it was time to select the valedictorian. That honor would be given to the graduating student who earned the highest grade point average in high school. The one thing that Betty had going against her was that she had made the commitment to her educational goals when she was in the tenth grade. Some students had made that commitment prior to their high school years and had worked successfully toward it.

After a couple of days, Betty found out that she was not selected because two other students had higher grade point averages. Betty was disappointed, but she was still happy that she ranked number three out of 100 graduating seniors. This was definitely an achievement, considering from where she came.

Soon graduation day arrived. Betty and her mom stood looking in the mirror at her in her cap and gown. Tears welled up in both of their eyes as they reflected how far Betty had come to get to that moment. But it was a precious moment for which words were not necessary; the bond between mother and daughter said it all.

After they arrived at the auditorium where the graduation was to be held, Betty turned to her mother and hugged her.

"Without her encouragement," she thought, "I may not have made it to where I am today." Then Betty went to take her place in the line of graduating seniors as they prepared to walk down the aisle into the auditorium.

The ceremony proceeded very smoothly. After the valedictorian gave her speech, Mr. Merman walked up to the podium. He was about to present an award to the graduating senior who had achieved despite the odds.

With great pride in his voice, Mr. Merman said, "I am very honored to be here tonight to present this award. The student that was chosen for this award is certainly deserving of it. I have watched her progress for two and a half years and I can truly say that I'm impressed. The student who is most deserving of this award is. . .Betty Tate."

Betty could hardly believe it. Yes, she believed that she was deserving of the award and felt really good about winning it, but the thought of winning it just seemed. . .well, it was hard for her to explain.

The best part about it was that she had to make a short acceptance speech. As she was standing on the podium looking out at the audience, she felt over-whelmed.

"This evening I stand before you," she said, "honored that I have been chosen for this award. I share the joy of this award with each of you because each of you probably have had to overcome one or more obstacle in order to complete high school. Like many people, my obstacles were primarily negative mental attitudes. I stand before you tonight and say: Let us be overcomers and not be overcome by this world. I can do it. You can do it. We can do it. Thank you."

As Betty walked to her seat, row by row, all of the senior class stood up to applaud her. Betty noticed some of the students fighting back tears, while others openly wept. She knew many of the people from her senior class. She therefore knew what some of them had been through in order to graduate. They had encountered numerous uphill battles—but they made it. Her short speech must have brought back many memories. Graduation day would definitely be a day for Betty to remember the rest of her life.

After the graduation ceremony ended, Betty proudly escorted her mother to the reception where they both mingled with the other guests. Although her mother did not earn a high school diploma, she definitely had plenty of knowledge about life. She was able to learn from her mistakes and was able to teach Betty many valuable lessons.

When the reception was over, Betty and her mom headed back to her house. They walked slowly, hand in hand, focusing on the sights and sounds of the creatures of the night. They could see the lightning bugs as they swarmed around the pole; and they could also hear the crickets singing their familiar song. As they reflected on the events of the evening, they concluded that this night marked the end of one chapter in Betty's life and the beginning of another.

Betty spent the summer working as an aide in a science lab. She felt very blessed to have a job working in her field prior to entering college in the fall. Hands-on experience was definitely different from classroom learning. Betty had already decided that she would major in science in college. Through her grades, test scores, and the recommendations of her teachers, she had obtained a scholarship at a local college. She was thrilled by this because it was the college of her choice.

The days went by pretty fast for Betty. She really enjoyed her summer. She went out frequently with Betha, who turned out to be her best friend. A very special bond had developed between them. They went to the movies and roller skated, and did many other fun activities together. They were both going to the same college in the fall, so they had much to look forward to. They both dated boys occasionally, but there was no one serious in either one of their lives.

Ever since Betty and Dan parted, she had been experiencing a lingering sense of loss. No, it didn't put a hold on her life, but she still felt it. Dan was the first boyfriend that she had ever had. She always felt that they had a good relationship—until that fateful day when it ended. Anyway, life was still good to her regardless of whether Dan was a part of it or not.

Soon the day arrived that she was to register for college. While waiting in line, she was quite surprised to see Dan walking towards her. She was even more surprised by his physical appearance. Yes, he was still neatly dressed, but he looked really tired. He had deep lines underneath his eyes, which made him seem older. She had seen him at their senior prom with Laurie. At that time, she noticed that he did not seem really happy, but she felt since he was the one who made the decision to end their relationship, he should live with the consequences.

Now to see him again at the college she was going to attend was unbelievable. She had just assumed that he would attend college out of town, but his presence at registration meant that he was about to attend the same college she had chosen. She did not have time to think more about it, though; Dan was now in front of her.

"Betty," he nervously said, "I am really glad to see you. I have not had the chance to talk to you in a long time. Well, let me change that statement. I've had many opportunities to talk to you, but uh. . .uh. . .I was afraid. I had so much to say to you, but I didn't know how to say it. I know that I hurt you really bad and I'm sorry for it. I know that I really don't deserve a 'yes' answer to the question I'm about to ask you, but I'm asking for your forgiveness. Please, Betty. . .please. . . After you have registered for your classes, come and have lunch with me. I would really like to talk to you again."

While he was talking, Betty was thinking about what he was saying. Her first reaction was one of bitterness. "Who does he think he is," she thought, "to think that he can come back into my life whenever he wants? Well, I will definitely tell him off."

Before she could say anything, memories of her past came flowing back to her. "Here I am," she thought, "getting ready to tell him off, yet I too, have made choices in my life that have hurt other people. Now here I am condemning Dan. At least I could go to lunch with him to hear what he has to say. He sounds really sincere."

She then agreed to meet him after she registered. He told her that he was going to go to the bookstore to purchase a book that he had forgotten on his list. They agreed to meet for lunch at one o'clock at The Hole, a fast food place on campus. While walking over to The Hole after she had registered, Betty experienced a wild rush of emotions, ranging from anger to happiness. She had not found again the kind of closeness that she and Dan had experienced. Yes, she had really missed him being a part of her life, but she knew that she could not accept him back on his parents' terms. She wondered what he could possibly want with her. "Suppose he wants us to get back together," she thought. "Would Laurie still be a part of his life?"

Well, she didn't have to wonder for long, for upon entering The Hole, she saw Dan already sitting at the booth waiting for her.

"Hi," he said. "I had this feeling that you'd changed your mind about meeting me. I wouldn't blame you if you did."

"I said I'd meet you. Besides, it's only 12:59," she replied.

"I know," he said, "but I still had my doubts about you showing up. What would you like to order, Betty? From what I have been told, they're suppose to have some terrific burgers and shakes here."

After they viewed the menu, they both ordered a double-decker hamburger, large fries, and a strawberry milk shake. As he put ketchup on his burger, Dan said, "I can't forget about the special bond that we had. You will never realize how much I missed you. I meant it when I apologized to you earlier." Dan hardly paused long enough for Betty to respond. He was eager to clarify his status with Laurie. "As you know, I continued dating Laurie in order to please my parents, but it just didn't work out. I knew that it wouldn't anyway. You were always on my mind, not Laurie or any other girl. I should not have yielded to my parents' insistence that I break it off with you. I did though, and I can't turn back the hands of time, so the only thing I can do is to hope that you can forgive me. It's still difficult for me to understand why my parents were so hard on you. I was raised to accept all people, yet they couldn't accept me dating you. I want you back regardless of how my parents feel. They didn't judge you by your inner being, for if they had, they would have seen exactly what I do—a very beautiful person inside and out. I'm sure that in time they'll learn to accept you as my girlfriend. And if they don't, well, I don't know. . ..We'll just have to deal with it."

"Dan," she began, "I have missed you a whole lot too, but it would be foolish for me to say that everything is okay between us. I need you to explain some more things to me. First of all, I would like to know how you feel about your parents' reasons for your breaking off with me. In other words, do you think I will be a hindrance to you since our backgrounds differ?"

"Thinking about it," he said, "I don't feel our backgrounds really differ. Sure, I was raised with all the material comforts that I could possibly want, whereas you were not, but the most important thing is that we share similar values, like honesty and trust. My parents raised me to regard a person's values more than anything else. I guess that they somehow lost track of what was really important. Perhaps they had a different picture of the girl I should date. I really don't know."

"I agree with you, Dan," said Betty. "I'm still concerned, though. If you believed all of that, then why did you break it off with me in the first place? I really don't understand that. You told me once before that your parents wanted you to continue dating Laurie, but that you didn't want to. From what you've told me, they didn't try to pressure you into continuing to date her, yet you did."

"That's very true," he said, "but this time my parents felt they had to take drastic measures 'in order to save me from myself,' to use their own words. They honestly did not mean any harm, for they truly believed they were doing the right thing. They told me that they would not pay for me to go to college if I didn't break off with you, since, in their view, I would be throwing my life away by dating you. Betty, you see, I made the wrong choice. But now I have decided that I would do better working my way through college rather than giving you up. My parents call this puppy love, but to me it's more than that. It's hard to explain, but there's just something special about you."

"I'm quite flattered," said Betty. "But still, how do I know that you won't change your mind again? I don't have the time nor the patience to play games. Besides that, I love myself too much to be at your beck and call. I definitely want you to understand this. You know that I have missed you, too—a whole lot. When you walked out of my life, I thought it was forever. To think that we are actually sitting here talking to one another now is unbelievable. We all make mistakes, so I am willing to forgive you and I am willing to start all over again."

"Betty," he said, "this is where trust comes in. I know that trust has to be earned and I am willing to do what it takes to earn your trust back."

Betty smiled and reached across the table, putting both of her hands into his. That moment a new awakening occurred between Dan and Betty. For them, it meant a new start and a different approach to their relationship. They rediscovered each other when all seemed lost. At last, they were together. In their minds, it was forever.

CHAPTER 8

Moving On Up

Before leaving The Hole, Dan told Betty that he would talk to his parents that day about them dating again. Out of respect for them, he felt that they should know. He also felt that they should know about his decision to work his way through college. In fact, he had already applied for and received a student loan, which he didn't have to start repaying until six months after graduation. He had also found a job on campus working for security. The job didn't pay much, but at least it would help to offset some of his college expenses. He really didn't know what their reactions would be, but he knew that he had to make some decisions on his own.

As Dan headed home, Betty went to the financial aid office to apply for a work-study job on campus. She hoped that they had a job opening at The Hole. She had decided while eating lunch that she would like to work as a waitress there. She had talked to one of the waitresses before leaving The Hole, and she told her all about the pay and the working environment.

When she got to the financial aid office, she looked at all of the job openings on the board. "Great!" she thought, as she saw the listing for a waitress at The Hole. According to the posted description, the job had the flexible hours that she wanted. She got an application from the receptionist and filled it out at the table. It didn't take her long, for she had no job experience. This would be her first job. After filling it out, she took it to The Hole. The manager's name was Mr. Hitt. He briefly looked at her application.

"Uh, huh, I see," he said in a very gruff voice, "you don't have any job experience. Several other people with job experience have given me their application. Why should I hire you when I can hire someone with the necessary experience?"

"Yes, Mr. Hitt," said Betty, "It's true I do not have any job experience as a waitress, but I can do the job. You see, I am a very hard worker, and also one that you can depend on. I want to work here because I like the atmosphere. Yes, I realize that a lot of hard work is involved and this job would be a challenge to me since I would have to be trained. I am used to challenges in my life and they surely do not scare me."

Mr. Hitt began to laugh. He laughed so hard that tears started rolling down his face. "You got a whole lot of spunk and I really like that. I'm old enough to be your father, but you really remind me of myself when I was your age. The other people I interviewed had experience, but they sure didn't have your spunk. I like your attitude, so I will hire you."

"Thank you," cried Betty. "You won't be sorry either." He asked Betty when she could start working. He was pleased when he found out that she could start right away, after she called her mom to let her know where she was. After that, he told her about her duties and exactly what he expected from her. Then she began to work at what she regarded as her first job, for she did not view the week working with her mom at Mrs. Bell's as a real job.

Today she was to only work five hours since it was her first day. By the time she left work, she was tired, but it was a good tired feeling. She felt good because she had learned everything she needed to in order to do her job well. She gathered her belongings and headed to the bus stop, which was about a half mile from The Hole.

"One thing for sure," she thought, "I could definitely use a car now. This walk can be very tiresome, especially after a long day at work."

She had taken driver's education at school, but had not yet received her license. She couldn't ask her mom for any help in purchasing a car because all of her money went to trying to meet the family's needs. Extra money was unheard of as far as her budget went. Her main concern was trying to make it week by week. She definitely would not be making enough money at The Hole to afford a car payment.

"Oh well," she thought. "I've been without a car for this long, so I know that I can make it with or without one, even though I know that a car would make it easier for me."

Much to her surprise, Dan was at the bus stop waiting for her when she arrived.

"Hi again," he said with a big grin on his face. "I thought you would like a ride home."

"I would love a ride home," said Betty. "It's definitely better than waiting for the bus. How did you know where I was? You didn't know that I had a job when you left after lunch."

"I called your mom," he responded. "She told me. So here I am. Besides that, I really don't like you waiting at the bus stop. Think about the weather; it could be raining or snowing, you never can tell."

"That's true," she answered. "I was thinking about having a car while I was walking to the bus stop. But right now, I know I can't afford one. Regardless of how the weather is, I will do what I have to. I can't let the weather stop me. I have come too far to stop now. Enough about that, for I want to hear about what happened when you told your parents that we were dating again."

"I was quite surprised by their reaction," said Dan. "Remember how I told you that I wasn't sure how they would react? I was not prepared for the positive reaction that I got from them. I was really taken aback by their reaction. They told me they noticed that I had been really unhappy since our breakup. They mistakenly believed that they were doing the best thing for me and that, as time passed by, I would realize it. They also realized that they were wrong about you."

"Yes, they liked you as a person," Dan continued, "but you just didn't have the proper background. They realized that everything I had told them about your inner beauty was true and more important than your social class. They taught me that the character of a person was more important than the social class. They just never realized that their only child would be interested in someone without the so-called 'proper background.' However, they have learned a very important lesson from this. They have learned that just like many people, they were able to 'talk the talk,' but were unable to 'walk the walk.' Well, anyway, my parents want to personally apologize to you and your mom. They want to know if both of you can come to dinner this weekend."

"I am surprised too," she said, "very pleasantly surprised, at that. Wonders definitely never cease. I will have to ask my mom and let you know about coming to dinner."

"I know that your mom will be surprised," he laughed. "When she recognized my voice over the phone, she was shocked. She asked me if I was Dan. When she found out that it was me, she was not pleased at all. I then explained to her how I felt about you and what a big mistake I had made before. At least she listened to what I had to say. But you know what? She warned me that I'd better not mess around with her baby anymore, or else I'll have to answer to her. I pretty much reassured her, so everything is fine."

"Well, I will talk to Mom," said Betty. "I can imagine her reaction to hearing from you again."

When they arrived at Betty's house, her mom had not yet come home from work. It was about a 40-minute ride on the bus from her job to home.

"Your mom will be home in about 10 minutes," said Dan while looking at his watch. "How about if we go to the bus stop and wait until her bus arrives? Then we can all walk back together. It's a beautiful night, and this way we can both ask her about dinner this coming weekend at my house."

"That's fine," Betty said. "My feet don't feel as tired now. The ride home really did relax me. In fact, I feel like I could walk a hundred miles now."

"Then let's go," he said as he reached for her hand.

They walked hand in hand to the bus stop. Soon after they started walking, they saw the bus approaching them. In a few minutes, it came to a stop and off got Betty's mom.

"Well, hello there you two," she said. "This is a pleasant surprise, seeing both of you at the bus stop waiting for me. So you tell me, what's up?"

"My parents invited you and Betty to dinner this coming weekend. Betty said that she would check with you first. I drove her home from work, so we decided to walk to the bus stop and check with you."

"This is really quite interesting to me," said her mom. "Sure. Why not? What evening would you like us to come this weekend?"

"My parents told me either day would be fine with them," said Dan.

"How about Saturday—that is, if it's a good time for Betty. What about at five o'clock?"

Betty nodded her head in agreement to what her mom had said.

"Great," said Dan, "I will tell my parents. They're really looking forward to meeting you, Miss Tate. I'll come and pick you two up at about 4:30, so you won't have to take the bus."

By then, they were at Betty's house. Her mom went inside the house while Betty and Dan said their good-byes.

Betty was so busy with college and working at The Hole that the days went by really fast. Soon it was Saturday, the day that they were going to Dan's house for dinner. Betty's mom seemed more excited than Betty that she was going to dinner. She had gotten up early Saturday morning and washed and curled her hair. She had even polished her nails, which she had not done for years.

"Betty," she said, "I feel really good. It seems like ages since I have taken the time to fix up myself. I feel like a different person. No, I feel like my old self again. I have shed my cocoon."

"Mom," said Betty, "I'm glad. I want you to be happy. You have done so much for me. You did without plenty of times just so I could have. You deserve to be happy. I really can't remember the last time that you fixed up yourself and went out. You really should do this more often. Have you thought about dating again?"

"Girl," her mom said, "you are really something else. It's kind of funny to think that you are asking me about dating. Me—going out on a date. I really can't picture myself going out on one. It's been so long. I have always been so busy trying to make ends meet for us that I never really thought about dating. You know what, though? What I would really like to do is to get my high school diploma. When I was a child, I had dreams of becoming a nurse. But as you can see, none of those plans worked out. I really get pleasure from seeing you go to college. You know, you are the first one on my side of the family to ever complete high school, and to think now that you are in college!"

"Mom," cried Betty, "I know that you can still do it. You have always encouraged me to go for my dreams. It's not too late for you. I can help you study for the GED test so you can get your diploma."

"I'm going to do it," her mom said excitedly, "I'm going to do it! There is absolutely no reason why I shouldn't. I can go to school during the day since

I work in the evening. I've talked to you many times about following after your dreams and never giving up, and yet I gave up. I don't know exactly why I did. Maybe it was fear, but now I will put that fear behind me. On Monday, I will check into getting my diploma."

"I'm really happy for you," said Betty. "Well, we can talk about this later. We need to hurry up and finish getting ready. Dan will be here soon. My— how fast time passes when you're with one of your favorite people."

Within a few minutes, they heard the doorbell ring. When Betty answered the door, Dan was standing outside. She invited him inside to wait, for they were not quite ready. Then Betty rushed back into her bedroom to finish getting dressed. Both Betty and her mom walked out of their bedrooms at about the same time to go downstairs.

"Well. . .well. . .well," Dan exclaimed as he watched mother and daughter walk down the stairs. "I see that I'm escorting two beautiful women tonight. Now tell me, which one of you happens to be the mom and which one the daughter?" he joked.

Betty's mom laughed and said, "Boy, don't you try to fool an old lady like me. I have been around a long time now, long before you were born."

"It's hard for me to tell," he said with a big grin on his face. "You may have been around long before me, but you sure don't look like it."

They left the house in a very light-hearted mood, laughing and talking all the way to Dan's house. When they arrived at his house, his parents were waiting on the porch to greet them.

"We are so glad that both of you could come," said Mr. Allen. "We were really looking forward to both of you coming."

"Yes, we were," said Mrs. Allen. "We strongly believe that we owe not only Betty an apology, but you also, Miss Tate."

"Please. . .please," said Betty's mom, "Mr. and Mrs. Allen, I want you both to call me by my first name, Estella."

"I agree with you," said Mrs. Allen, while Mr. Allen also nodded his head in agreement. "There is really no sense in us being so formal with one another. Miss Tate. . .uh, I mean Estella, you can call me Jeanette and my husband's name is Alfred. Now, I have something more to say to you, Betty, and to you, Estella. Even though I am going to say it, it's from Alfred and me. Betty, our son is happy being with you. His happiness is far more important to us than anything else. You are not doing any harm to him, in fact you are good for him. Yes, I know what we said before. But we were wrong—very, very wrong. Forgive both of us, will you?"

"I really do understand why you did what you did," said Betty. "No, I didn't like it. But I do understand. You did what you thought was best for Dan. I know that my mom does what she feels is best for me. The most important thing is that we learn and grow from our experiences. I know that I have."

"I agree with Betty," said her mom. "I've tried to teach Betty that she has choices in life. The choices that she makes could affect her entire life. The most important thing is that if she finds out that she has made the wrong choice, she should admit it, then try to change it. Jeanette, you and Alfred have done this; so all is forgiven. It takes a lot sometimes to admit that you are wrong. Let us just put what happened where it belongs, and that is in the past. Let's just have a good time tonight."

Everyone agreed to having a good time, and that they did. Dan's mom and Betty's mom found out that they had some things in common. They both knew how to sew and crochet. Betty's mom could even knit. Years ago, she had a desire to be a nurse and also to use her talent for making things with her hands. She was so talented that she did not even need a pattern to make anything. She always had a desire to make and sell her own creations, but she could not see how it could be done. She did not have the money nor the business knowledge that she needed to have her own business.

Dan's mom had the same desire. She was a college professor, so she just simply did not have the time to run a business. She knew what it took to run a successful business, for she taught business courses to college students, as well as other people who were interested in starting a business.

"This is really interesting," said Dan's mom. "We both have the same interest in making things and having our own business. I would really like to see some of your work sometime. Would you like to see some of mine?"

"Yes, I would love to see some of your work," said Betty's mom as Jeanette got up from the chair. She left the room briefly and came back with a big bag full of things that she had made. Betty's mom was very impressed by her work.

"I see that you are very good," she told Jeanette.

"I am really very impressed by your work. You are as good as I am."

"I have the money to invest in a business, but I just don't have the time to run it. I love my job as a professor, so I definitely won't quit it. I have thought many times to invest in a business and to get someone to run it for me. If I do this, you can bring some of your work into the shop to be sold. Of course, I have to like your work and I would have to get a certain percentage of what you sold. We can talk about the fine details of it later, when and if I decide to do it. The terms would be fair and satisfactory to both of us, though."

"That's fine," said Betty's mom. "Right now I am going to concentrate on getting my high school diploma and becoming a nurse."

The evening passed by so quickly that no one realized how late it was until the grandfather clock bonged 12 times, signaling that it was midnight.

"Oh wow," said Betty, "we didn't mean to stay this long. We didn't realize just how late it was getting."

"That's okay," said Mrs. Allen. "We didn't realize how late it was either. We have really had a great time talking."

"Well, we're going to say our goodbyes now, for it is quite late," said Betty's mom. "We did have a good time and perhaps we can get together again."

They all said their goodbyes to each other. Dan drove Betty and her mom back home and walked them to their door. After they said their good-byes, he headed home. The remainder of the weekend passed by pretty fast for all, for they were busy preparing themselves for Monday.

Monday morning came. Betty's mom was excited, for today she would check into getting her high school diploma. She made a few calls until she found out where she had to go to apply to take the GED test. She found out that she had to take a six-week refresher course before she was allowed to take the test. The course was offered during the day. This was perfect for her, since she worked in the evening. She was nervous about it, but she knew that she had to do it in order to better her life. She decided to go to the school and register right away.

After she had finished registering, she felt a sense of fulfillment, even though this was only the beginning to the long journey ahead of her. She felt like a little girl again; she couldn't wait to tell Betty that she had actually signed up. She knew within herself, as she had told Betty so many times, that she had to believe in herself no matter how bleak the situation looked. Within herself, she knew she'd make it.

While Betty's mom started her day by registering for class, Betty was going from class to class. She was really enjoying her classes. She definitely saw the difference between college and high school. In college, the work was more difficult and the professors expected more from you. In high school, if a student missed a certain amount of days, the truant officer would investigate to find out why. In college, it was entirely up to each student to make it to class and to do the required work. The professor did not beg and plead with the students to make it to class or to do their work. The rule was very simple: If you didn't do your work, you would flunk. If you wanted to waste your time and money by flunking out, it was really up to you. Betty was so glad she'd learned to discipline herself to study during high school. Because of this, she didn't have such a big adjustment to make during college.

Dan and Betty had made a date to meet for lunch after their last class. Their last class ended at the same time, which was perfect timing. After lunch she had to go straight to work. She had finally decided to work only five hours per day at the Hole instead of eight hours. Her school work was the number one priority for her. She could make it working only five hours, even though eight would have definitely been better. Dan also had to go to work at his security job after lunch. Even though his parents had relented and were paying his way through school, he had decided to keep his job. He was only working five hours per day also, so he was able to take Betty home each day that she worked.

After Betty's last class, she walked on down to The Hole, where Dan was going to meet her for lunch. They noticed one another at the same time. Dan was already there and had found a secluded booth away from the crowd of other students. He turned around at about the same time she was entering the door.

"Betty, Betty," he said excitedly. "I have some really good news for you and your mom. My mom is going to call your mom when she gets off work tonight and tell her, if she hasn't already. You know that my mom wants to open her own business, but she doesn't have the time to run it. After you two left early Sunday morning, my mom and dad talked about this some more. They both decided that this is as good a time as ever for my mom to do it. She has the business know-how, plus she knows of a shop that has been on the market for many months now. She believes that she can get a good price on it.

She will have to hire someone as a cashier, but this shouldn't be any problem. She will do everything else. Anyway, she wants to look at some of the things that your mom has made. If she likes them, she will put them in her shop to sell. This way, they both will make money. If the shop is a big success, then there are endless possibilities for them."

"This is really great," said Betty. "My mom wouldn't have to quit school to do this, plus she could still go on and become a nurse. I know that your mom will like my mom's work, for she is good. I wonder if she knows yet."

"You know, we really shouldn't tell your mom," he said. "Let's just wait until my mom calls her. Then she'll be surprised!"

"Good idea," said Betty. "But I can't wait to see her face after your mom tells her."

They ate lunch in silent anticipation of what was to come. Afterwards, they both headed on to their jobs to begin working. After Betty's shift ended, she went outside to wait by the door for Dan. The cool breeze felt so good. She bent down to take off her shoes, for her feet were aching from standing up so long. As she stood back up, she saw Dan walking towards her.

"Hi," he said. "I see that you have aching feet tonight. We don't have to walk far to the car. I know that your aching feet really anticipated that."

"Yes. . .yes. . .yes," she said, "Tonight I really feel burnt out, but I am so-o-o-o happy. Just think—if I had dropped out of high school when I wanted to, this would probably be my life's work. I see the light now. Like the song goes, 'I once was lost, but now I'm found.'

"I am so glad," said Dan as he bent to kiss her on the cheek.

"You are glad," Betty teased. "Well, think about how my aching feet feel."

They walked to the car in a happy mood. When Dan arrived at Betty's house, he decided to go inside to see if Betty's mom would mention his mom's business. When they walked inside the house, Betty's mom was sitting at her sewing machine making a table scarf from a pretty white lacy material.

"Mom, Mom," cried Betty. "You must know already. Also, you and Dan's mom must have been able to come to a mutual agreement on the terms. I just knew that she would like your work. Oh Mom, I am so proud of you. Also, didn't you go to enroll for class today?"

"Yes," she said, "We were able to agree on the terms of her selling my items in her shop. Jeanette is making an offer on the shop today. She is sure that she will get it because the shop has been on the market for awhile now. I'm getting started now so I can have plenty to sell on opening day. I'll still be able to study to take my GED. I'm really not worried about it. You did it. So can I."

"I know that you can do it," said Betty. "I definitely know this as a fact."

"I know this to be true too," said Dan. "You and Betty are definitely achievers. You may have been sidetracked, but now there is no stopping either one of you."

"You are right about that," Betty and her mom said at the same time. "We definitely are going to make it."

In the brightly lit room, mother and daughter affirmed their beliefs in themselves and each other. Mother and daughter—both in unison and both working towards the fulfillment of their dreams. It was a very beautiful moment to be relished, and one that would be etched forever in their memories.

Time passed and the handicraft shop became a big success. Betty's mom had taken the GED test and passed it with flying colors. What a celebration they had, for it was indeed a dream come true. Now her mom was enrolled in a community college, taking courses toward becoming a registered nurse. She had a long way to go, but she was determined to make it. The fact that she was an older college student in comparison to most of the other students did not deter her. In fact, it made her work harder. She had a dream and she was going all the way.

Finally, the day came when Betty and her mom were able to move from their old neighborhood to a house in a better neighborhood. No, it wasn't a huge house, but it was what they wanted. Besides, they were buying it instead of renting it. With the income from the handicraft shop, they were able to get a fairly new house. It had two bedrooms, two baths, a den, a living room, and a spacious kitchen. They were really excited over the prospect of moving out of their old neighborhood.

Both of them had decided that they would only move their beds to their new home. The other furniture was so worn that it wasn't worth renting a truck to move it. For the time being, bean bags would suffice until they could afford more furniture. One thing for sure was that neither one of them wanted to get deep in debt buying furniture. It would take time for them to furnish the entire house, but at least they were living in a home that was their own.

Betty laughed when she thought about eating at their old table and how she had to sit very still in order not to shake it. The legs were so wobbly that if she shook the table, it would have fallen down. Sitting on a bean bag while eating would definitely be more comfortable than trying to hold up a table while eating.

After the two beds were moved out of the old house, Betty lingered awhile for one last look. This had been her home for so long. She and her mom had shared a lot of happy memories there. Now to think that she was actually moving from it. The prospect of never returning there again was actually difficult for her to take. However, as time went on, she would only have faded memories of it.

She walked through every room of the house slowly. After she finished walking through it, she went outside and stood on the porch. She saw the familiar big oak tree with Albert, Louise, and Johnny underneath it. Betty walked from the porch over to the big oak tree to say good-bye to them.

"Betty," said Louise, "we see that you are moving on up in this world. You are moving out of this rat hole. I envy you, yet I am very happy for you and your mom. When your mom told me that she was going to college, I nearly freaked out. She is doing everything that I want to do. Just maybe, I'll get my life together. It seems impossible in the natural, but you and your mom are doing it so. . .I don't know."

"Yeah," said Albert in a wistful tone. "You two are really moving away from here. You know, I can still remember the day when you told us you were planning to drop out of school. Each time I see you I probably will mention this to you. Girl, you've come a long way!"

"That's right," Johnny said. "You've come a long way. Don't forget us, Betty. Come back and see us sometimes. Just maybe. . .when you come back, one or all of us will have our lives straightened out. Well anyway, good luck to you."

Betty walked away from the big oak tree after telling each one them good-bye. However, Betty felt that regardless of where she moved or how far she climbed the social ladder, the big oak tree would always be a part of her past; a past that helped her to become the person that she was at that moment. She was now experiencing a new awakening. She was moving away from her past—to another house, to a different way of life--but she would never forget where she came from.

CHAPTER 9

What Is and What Could Have Been

B etty and Dan continued to date throughout the college years. Toward the end of their third year, Dan finally asked Betty to marry him. She wasn't really surprised, for she knew it would be forthcoming. They had become closer and closer over the years. They decided to wait until they finished college and settled into a job before they got married. When they announced their engagement to their parents, they too were not surprised, but very excited.

As the end of their last year of college approached, Betty and Dan received job offers. This was exciting to them. Now they could go ahead and set a wedding date. They decided to set the date for August 9th, exactly two months after they graduated from college. Now—since they had actually set a date—it was time to start making plans.

Both of their moms were very excited about helping to make the wedding plans. Neither one of them had ever had a wedding themselves, so they wanted to help make this a very special day for Betty. Betty's mom had never been married and Dan's mom was married by a judge in a courthouse, so they decided to go all out for Betty and Dan. This would be a day that both Betty and Dan would always remember. Betty and both of the moms decided to meet the next day for lunch. Betty wanted to pick out her wedding dress, so they decided to meet downtown for lunch since all of the best bridal shops were located there. They decided to meet at Louie's.

Betty was the first one to arrive. Since she did not see them, she found a seat close to the bay window and awaited their arrival. Soon after that, both of the moms came in together laughing and talking. While looking at her mom walk in through the door, Betty could not help thinking about how much her appearance had changed in recent months. No more did her mom wear drab, loose-fitting clothes. No more did she wear her hair brushed straight back off her face. Today she had on a colorful, flowery dress and her hair was cut and styled in a way that enhanced her features. She now had the air of someone who was very confident and very secure in who she was and what she wanted to be.

"Betty," said her mom as she took a seat across from her in the booth, "I made it. I thought I'd be late. I got so caught up in studying that I almost forgot the time."

"Well," said Dan's mom, "at least we all made it, plus we're all on time. Let's go ahead and order. While we're eating, Betty, you can tell us exactly what kind of wedding dress you're looking for. Also, we need to discuss who else you want in your wedding party. For example, who will be your bridesmaids?"

"I've always dreamed of getting married in a white lacy gown with a long train. I don't quite know what I want, but when I see it, I'll know for sure."

"Okay, first things first. Let's order," said Betty's mom as she picked up the menu, "I am so hungry."

They each picked up a menu and viewed it for awhile. By the time they'd finished looking at it, a waitress came over to take their orders. It didn't take long before she came back with three plates of food. The food looked and smelled really good. Not only that, but they soon discovered that the food tasted as good as it looked and smelled.

"Now," said Betty as she put down her fork, "I want to have two bridesmaids, a ring bearer, a train bearer, and, of course, a maid of honor. I'm going to ask Betha to be one of my bridesmaids. Regarding my maid of honor, there's only one person that I would even consider asking. She is very special to me, and that person is you, Mom."

"You know that I am honored to be your maid of honor, Betty," she said as she reached over and gave her hand a squeeze. "You know what, though? Who are you going to ask to give you away?"

"I don't know yet," said Betty. "I wish my father was here to give me away in marriage. I know he'd have loved Dan as much as I do. I will have to think about that later. Right now, I'd like to find my wedding dress."

They finished eating and then headed on to the first bridal shop on their list. Since it was the largest one, they were really hoping to find a dress there.

"I see a lot of dresses I like," said Betty while walking around looking, "but I don't see the dress with the neckline that I want. Here's another dress I like, but it's still lacking in what I want."

"Don't despair," said Dan's mom. "We still have a lot of other stores on our list. Remember, this is only the first store. This is the largest one, but smaller ones may have a good selection, too."

"You're right," said Betty. "Let's leave this store and go on to another one."

They made their exit, then went to store after store. The results were the same.

"What are we doing?" cried Betty's mom. "The solution to this is very simple. Betty cannot find a dress with everything that she wants on it, so the only thing to do is make the dress ourselves! Betty, make out a list of everything that you want on your dress. Then draw a picture of it. We can make it."

"I can definitely help, too," said Dan's mom excitedly.

Betty agreed to this, so they all left and went their separate ways. Betty was going to get exactly what she wanted in a gown, and it was going to be made by two women who loved her very much. The wedding plans proceeded as Betty and Dan went on to complete their last year of college. On Betty's graduation day, Betty and her mom both got up early and took a long walk together through their neighborhood. They reflected on their past life and where they were now.

"Betty," said her mom, "today will be yet another chapter ending in your life and the beginning of another. In a couple of months, you will be getting married and moving from our home to be with your new husband. I'll miss you, but I am really happy for you. You have really worked hard to achieve your goals. Tell me, Betty, years ago when you were working toward your goals, did you sometimes feel like calling it quits when the going got real rough?"

"Yes," said Betty. "At times I felt like giving up. But deep within myself I knew that I couldn't. Mom, I just didn't want to give up on my life. Giving up to me would mean not following after my dreams. You know, I used to put a whole lot of emphasis on money. My outlook has changed somewhat. Yes, I know that you must have money for material goods in life, but you know what, Mom? I only wanted money to satisfy my urges to get everything that I wanted materially... clothes, a car, the ability to stay upon the latest trends, and above all, the chance to say that I have this, this and that."

"Mom," Betty continued, "I saw the people in my neighborhood always needing and wanting for material goods. I was determined not to be like them. I could have turned to crime by stealing or selling drugs, but Mom, I didn't want to do anything illegal to achieve my dreams. I realize now that the more a person gets materially, the more that person wants. As time goes on, that person may or may not put money in its proper perspective and realize that the greatest satisfaction in life is not how much money you possess, but being happy about who you are and being secure about it. Some people never put money in its proper perspective, though. They live their lives only for achieving material goods. I think it's very sad, and I'm so glad that I've put money in its proper perspective."

"You're so right," said her mom. "You have grown, Betty, in so many ways. I am really proud of how you've turned out."

"Thank yourself also, Mom," said Betty. "You've been a big inspiration to me. Even though I'll be getting married in a few months, I'll still come by and visit you, and you are always welcome to visit me. This is not the end of our relationship just because I am getting married. You are and always will be my mom."

Mother and daughter walked back home together, reflecting on their past and eagerly looking forward to their future.

Graduation day went by very smoothly for Betty and Dan. They both graduated with honors. In fact, Dan ranked number five and Betty ranked number four out of a class of 250 graduating seniors. Betty received her degree in science, while Dan got his in secondary education. They had both decided that they would start work right away. They had two months before the wedding, so they wanted to save as much money as they could. Betty had a job working as a supervisor in a lab and Dan was teaching summer school until school started in the fall. His permanent teaching job was to start after they came back from the honeymoon.

After Betty's first day on the job, she knew that she had chosen the right job and the right field. She loved working in the lab. It was interesting as well as challenging.

"What more could I ask for?" she thought to herself. "I have a wonderful job, a great fiancé, and a beautiful life overall."

Her mind drifted to the big oak tree and the familiar faces always under it. She thought about the other people she knew who had dropped out of school and were now doing nothing with their lives. After work that day, she decided to drive back to her old neighborhood to see if the same familiar faces were under the big oak tree. The last time she went back to visit, they were still there, talking the same old talk of what they could have done and giving excuses for why they hadn't. "Maybe, just maybe," she thought, "they won't be there. Maybe they've gotten their lives together."

After work she jumped into her car to leave for her old neighborhood. Yes, she had a car and was driving now. She was able to buy it during her last year of college. It was a small car, but it definitely served its purpose. No more waiting at the bus stop—plus, Dan didn't have to take her places anymore. That was a part of her past and she was never planning on returning to it. She really enjoyed the freedom of just getting in her car and going places. Betty's mom had also learned to drive and now owned a car.

Although Betty was very happy now with her life, just thinking about the people she knew from her past saddened her. Once she got to her old neighborhood, she drove slowly and looked around. Her old neighborhood seemed as if it had deteriorated even more since the last time she'd been there. She saw a gang of teenagers hanging on the street corner, smoking and gawking at each car that went by. She saw her old house. Two little children were playing in the dirt in the front yard. Part of the wooden porch had sunk down. On the part that had not sunk was an old chair. Sitting in it was a plump older lady with an old red polka dot scarf tied around her head. Her clothes were old and worn and she had on red thongs.

"She looks familiar," thought Betty. "I doubt if I know her, though. She looks about ten years older than me. She still looks familiar, though."

Betty parked her car by the big oak tree. She saw Albert and Johnny standing underneath it.

"Hi," she called out as she got out of the car. "How are you two doing?"

"We're doing fine," said Johnny. "It's really good to see you again. The last time you stopped by was about two months ago. I can see that you're still looking real good. Do you still have the same boyfriend that you had the last time that you stopped by? I'd like to take his position."

"Johnny, be for real," said Albert. "What would Betty want with someone like you? She's a career woman now."

Before Johnny could say anything, Betty said, "Thanks for the compliment Johnny, but I'll be getting married in less than two months. By the way, where is Louise? She's not ill is she?"

"I see that you've not heard the good news about Louise," said Johnny. Louise doesn't hang out with us anymore. She's getting her act together. You know that she wanted to become a doctor. Well, she took the GED test and she passed it. She's now enrolled in a community college, majoring in pre-medicine. She's got a long way to go, but she's determined to make it."

"Yeah," said Albert. "The girl has actually left us. It's hard to believe sometimes. She told me that you and your mom were a great influence on her. We miss her, but we're really proud of her. Maybe we can get our lives together, so the next time you come around you won't see us hanging around. You know what, though? We have someone else who has taken Louise's place. She lives in your old house. In fact, she's sitting on the front porch now. You know her. Look for yourself."

Betty turned towards her old house. This time, the lady was getting up from her chair and walking down the steps. In fact, the lady was walking towards them.

"How do you figure that I know her?" said Betty, as she briefly turned back to Albert and Johnny. "She looks familiar to me, but that's it. Maybe I have seen her out somewhere."

"She should look familiar," said Johnny. "You don't recognize your old friend?"

By then, the lady was upon them. Betty and the lady looked at one another.

"Gabby," cried Betty, "Gabby, is it really you?"

The lady's eyes shifted from Betty towards the ground.

"Yes," she nervously said, "It's me, Betty."

"It's really great to see you again. It's been a long time."

Betty thought back on the past. Gabby had not spoken to her since their argument. In fact, she had gone out of her way to avoid Betty. She knew that Gabby had not finished high school. She heard through the school grapevine that Gabby had dropped out of school because she was pregnant. Even though she lived close to Gabby, she had very seldom seen her after their breakup. Now, to see her. . .now, looking at least ten years older than what she really was, and living in Betty's old house. Betty couldn't believe it!

"Uh," mumbled Gabby, "It's nice seeing you too, Betty." She still avoided eye contact with Betty. As

they were standing there, one of the children play-
ing in the yard came and held on to Gabby's leg.

"Mom, Mom," he cried, "I want something to eat.
Can I have a cracker?"

"Okay Lee," she said, "I'm coming."

"This must be your son, Gabby," said Betty. "I
saw him playing outside with another little boy. Is
he the only child that you have or do you have oth-
ers?"

For the first time since their meeting, Gabby
looked Betty directly in the eyes. She did not flinch,
but instead looked upon Betty in a hostile manner.
The question that Betty asked her had certainly
changed Gabby's manner from nervous to defiant.

"Both of the boys that you saw playing outside in
the yard are mine," she said boldly, "plus I have a
little baby girl asleep in the house. So what about it,
huh? What do you want to make of it, huh?"

Gabby," Betty said softly, "I didn't mean any harm
in asking about how many kids you have. Gabby,
we were best friends for many years. We shared a lot
of memories together. I mean no harm to you what-
soever, Gabby. I still care about you."

"So why did you come back to this neighborhood?"
asked Gabby. "You don't live here anymore, so why
do you bother coming back? Did you hear that I lived
in your old house and you came back to gloat about
it?"

"I still have friends who live in this neighborhood,"
said Betty. "Just because I have moved doesn't mean
that I have to give up my friends from my old neigh-
borhood. No, I didn't know you lived in my old house.
Think about how I was prior to our relationship end-

ing, Gabby. Was I the type to gloat because of what I had? No. . .no. . .Let me rephrase that sentence; I didn't have much myself as far as material possessions."

"Well," said Gabby in a less hostile voice, "you have made something out of your life now, and it's just sort of strange to me that you would come back to visit. I really don't view you as the type, though, to gloat over what you got. I'd like to talk to you before you leave, but first I have to go inside the house and get Lee something to eat. If you have the time, could you come and sit on the porch with me for a few minutes?"

"I have the time," said Betty. "In fact, I can walk over with you now."

Betty said good-bye to Albert and Johnny. Then she walked back to Gabby's house with her. When they got to the first step, Gabby stopped and opened her mouth as if she had something to say. She hesitated as if she didn't know how to say what she wanted.

"Betty," she said hesitantly. "Uh. . .uh. . .well, I would really prefer if you waited on the porch for me. I will be right back. Just let me go in and give Lee a few crackers. Uh, I would invite you in but you see, I. . .well. . .you know how it is."

"I understand," said Betty. "I'll just sit here and wait."

"What do you mean by saying that you understand," said Gabby, hostile once again. "It's a nice evening and I just think that it would be nicer sitting on the porch rather than inside the house."

"Gabby," said Betty in a perturbed tone, "I'm not here to argue with you. If you're going to make something negative from everything that I say, then it would be best if I left."

Betty turned and started to walk away. Gabby stood there and looked at her as she walked toward the car.

"Wait, Betty," cried Gabby. "Wait, please. This seems like a repeat of the incident that we had years ago. I realize that I am on the defensive, and I really don't have a reason to be. Betty, I really would like to talk with you. Will you please come back?"

"Yes," said Betty as she turned and walked back toward Gabby.

"Thanks," said Gabby. "Let me get Lee some crackers now. I'll be right back."

Then she went inside her house to get Lee his crackers. She was feeling more at ease with Betty. She realized years ago she was wrong in her attitude toward Betty, but she had too much pride to admit it. Betty had been the best friend that she ever had, but she lost her friendship because of her stupid pride.

When she first recognized Betty, she felt very awkward, for she was in old worn clothes and had a scarf tied around her head, while Betty was dressed in an expensive three-piece suit. Betty's hair was cut and styled in a way that was very becoming to her. Gabby saw her new car and felt inferior to Betty. She was the same age as Betty, yet she had made nothing out of her life, and to think that she was living in the house where Betty used to live. She had heard from Albert about Betty's accomplishments. She had even seen Betty's engagement announcement in the newspaper. Talking to Betty though, made Gabby realize that Betty had not turned into a snob. In fact, she really seemed interested in Gabby.

"Well, let me hurry back out," she thought to herself, "before Betty starts to wonder if I'm actually going to come back."

"I have a confession to make," said Gabby as she walked back on the porch. "I've thought about you for a long time. I was jealous of you when you first told me about your goals, mainly because I felt insecure about myself. Remember that I told you that you were no better than me. I was scared, Betty. You see, here you were, my best friend, telling me about what you wanted to achieve and you even had a plan on how to go about it. I didn't want you to do any more than I did. I wanted to feel like we were on equal footing. I couldn't stand the thought of you doing more than me. I was really hurt when you chose studying over me. I felt that you would change your mind eventually and come back to me. But you didn't. You hung in there. Well, here you are now. I can tell that you're happy with yourself and that you're not hurting for money. I only wish that I'd set goals for myself when I was younger. I didn't though, and look at where I am now in my life."

"I *am* very happy," said Betty. "But Gabby, it's not too late for you. It'll be a little difficult for you since you have three kids to look after, but you can make it. Louise is in college now and she has kids."

"That's true," said Gabby, "I kick myself everyday for not taking advantage of my education as you did. It was free, too. That's the worst part of it. I dropped out of school in my junior year. I was in love and I was three months pregnant. Remember

Joe Bitt? Well, I got married to him. He dropped out in his junior year also to get a job to support us. The only job he could find was in a gas station pumping gas. With the pressure of a young baby and the lack of money, the marriage lasted less than a year. Joe walked out on us. Before he walked out, I found out that I was pregnant with our second child. I was left with two kids, no husband, and no job skills. You think I would have learned, but here I am now with a baby girl by a different man."

Gabby began to cry. Betty went over and put her arms around her shoulder to comfort her.

"I know. . .[sniff] that it's [sniff] not too late," she cried, "but I have a long way to go. At times, it seems almost impossible, and I haven't even got started yet. I just have to do it, though, for myself, so I can be fulfilled as a person."

"You've got to believe you can achieve your dreams, Gabby," said Betty. "I say this because, more than likely, you'll run into obstacles. It could be someone trying to put you down for what you are trying to do with your life. If you don't believe in yourself, it will be easier for you to succumb to nega-tive feedback. Never, never give up. Once you do give up, then it's over."

Betty and Gabby sat on the porch and talked for several hours—two old friends reuniting, talking about what could have been and what was.

CHAPTER 10

A Blessed Union

The day of August 9th finally arrived. It was really a beautiful day—the day Dan and Betty would unite as man and wife. Betty had decided Dan's father would give her away. She had also asked Gabby to be her other bridesmaid, for they had became closer since their reunion.

Betty's mom was helping her to prepare for her wedding. They were both glowing with excitement. The limousine was due to arrive in about 30 minutes to take Betty and her mom to the church. "This is one of the happiest days of my life," she thought, as she viewed herself in the mirror. Her mom came and stood beside her.

"Betty," said her mom, "you really look ravishing standing there. This gown suits you."

It was indeed a beautiful gown. Betty's and Dan's mom had spent many hours sewing the gown. It was pure white with pearls encased in circles sewn all over it. The neckline was V-shaped and the string of white pearls that Dan's mom had given her accentuated the beautifully cut neckline.

Betty turned and took her mom's hand gently in hers and said, "Mom you have helped to make this day very special for me. I also want to thank you for being my maid of honor. You are indeed a very special friend as well as my mother."

"I am honored to be your maid of honor," replied her mom. "You will always—no matter where you go or who you are with—always have a special place in my heart."

Then her mom went to get Betty's suitcase. She put it by the door so the limousine driver could put it in the car. After the wedding ended, the limousine driver was going to take them to their reception at the country club, and then on to the airport where they would take a flight to Hawaii. They were planning to spend two weeks in Hawaii on their honeymoon before returning back home again. Their home was a two-bedroom townhouse, which their parents jointly made a down payment for them. When Betty and Dan tried to protest about this, their parents only told them that they knew that Dan and Betty could afford it themselves, but they wanted to help out. Besides that, Dan and Betty had only worked a couple of months and they needed all the money they could get to start off their married life. This was definitely an excellent start for them.

The doorbell rang. It was the limousine driver informing them of his arrival. He gathered up Betty's wedding train and her suitcase to put in the car. Then off they went, heading toward the church. It was about a 20-minute ride to the church, so Betty and her mom became very comfortable in their leather, cushioned seat.

"Well, fairy tales definitely come true," Betty thought, as she leaned her head back on the seat. "They don't come true like in the Cinderella tales. In the tales, the prince comes and takes Cinderella away and they live happily ever after. Real life is definitely not like that. With life comes awakenings, changes that can make you a stronger person or a totally defeated one."

Soon they arrived at the church and Betty and her mom hurried to the dressing room where they were met by Gabby and Betha. They both hugged Betty when she entered the room.

"We're already dressed," said Betha. "So let us help you put on your wedding train. Stand still while I help you put your hat on."

After Betha had finished, everyone stood back to view her in her entire wedding outfit. The wedding train was so long that it swirled around Betty five times. It definitely made a beautiful picture.

Just then, they heard the strains of the organ signaling that the wedding was about to take place. They all hugged Betty one last time before her mom put the veil over her face. Then they all got into their proper position, waiting to begin. Finally, the procession began. First went Betha, and then Gabby. Next came Betty's mom, and then the two little flower girls who strew rose petals all along the path Betty was going to walk down. Next came Gabby's son, Lee, the ring bearer.

Now it was time for Betty to enter. She walked to the entrance of the door and paused. Everyone stood up in honor of the soon-to-be bride. She began to walk slowly down the aisle. Directly in front of her, by the minister was Dan. Dan looked quite stunning in his black and gray tuxedo. While she was approaching him, he was looking directly at her. He, just like she, did not seem the least bit nervous. After all, both were looking forward to finally uniting as man and wife.

When Betty got beside Dan, they took each other's hand and turned toward the minister. They had decided to forego the traditional wedding vows and write their own.

"Betty and Dan," said the minister, "wrote their own vows to each other. First, we will listen to Dan's vows to Betty. Then Betty will say hers to Dan. You can begin now, Dan."

"Betty," said Dan, "since the first moment I saw you, I knew that you were a special person. Each moment I spent with you made me love you more and more. Betty, you are the light of my life. The day that you agreed to marry me made me the happiest man in the world. Now to know that in a few minutes we will finally be married makes me feel totally fulfilled as a person. I love you, Betty."

"Dan," Betty began, "words cannot accurately describe my love for you. It's like a tumultuous sea, a howling wind that continues on and on. You have shown me so much love. On the way over here, I thought about my life in comparison to a fairy tale. I have always believed that the 'living happily ever after' endings to fairy tales were unrealistic. I realized today that it really wasn't so unrealistic. It really depends on how you view obstacles in life. It's basically your total outlook on life. Dan, I know that we can have that happy ending in our lives together. We can and we will make it. I love you, Dan."

After they said their vows to each other, the minister turned to the audience and said, "Betty requested earlier that she be allowed to say a few words to her mom during the ceremony. Betty, your request is granted."

Betty turned to her mom and said, "Mom, you have been a mother and a father to me. You did without so I could have. I'm here today because of your love and your strength which helped me through the difficult times. The wisdom you have imparted to me will forever guide my life. Thank you, Mom, for everything."

Then Betty turned back to Dan, and the minister said, "We have all witnessed the vows between Dan and Betty. By the power invested in me, I now pronounce them man and wife. May God's blessings be always on their lives."

This marked the beginning of a new life together for Dan and Betty—a life together that would bring forth many awakenings. Yes, Dan and Betty had a fairy tale wedding. But for them, it was the beginning of "living happily ever after." They knew they would face many challenges in living together. With this attitude and a strong love for each other, they knew they would make it.

CHAPTER 11

Reflections

Within two years, a girl named Marie was born to Dan and Betty. The years passed quickly. Marie learned to walk and talk.

In what seemed like no time at all to Dan and Betty, she started school. Time continued to pass and Marie rapidly moved from grade school to high school.

One beautiful morning, Marie was slowly getting out of bed. Looking out of her window, she could see the chauffeur polishing her mother's silver antique car. She could see the squirrels running across the green lush yard, carrying nuts to and fro. Looking on past the house, she could see the stable man going to feed her horse.

Marie slowly turned from the window. She felt as if she had a big burden ahead of her, for today she was going to tell her mother and father that she wanted to drop out of school for she was now 16. She could not understand why she had to spend her time studying and doing her best in school since her grandparents and parents were financially well off. Besides, her grandparents had set up a trust fund for her when she was born, and she could have it when she turned 18.

Just then, Marie heard her mother's voice at the door, asking her to come and eat breakfast. Quickly she put on her clothes and hurried down to the kitchen. Marie had decided to tell her parents immediately after sitting down at the breakfast table.

"What could be so wrong about wanting to travel and see the world," she thought to herself as she sat at the breakfast table. "I can learn more from seeing the world than by being in school."

"Mom and Dad," Marie said nervously, as she buttered a piece of toast, "I want to drop out of school and just travel around the world. I'm 16 now, and I have to make some choices on my own pertaining to my life. We have money, so I really don't see the big deal about me having to finish school."

Betty looked down at her well-manicured hands. She thought about how hard she had worked to get to where she was. She thought about the many hours of studying and working during college. During those years, there were some nights she had slept only four hours. Yes, she had a very good job now, but she definitely worked hard for it. Now to hear her daughter talk about dropping out of school. . . She would just have to teach Marie the reality of the situation. She realized that Marie would have to go through many awakenings. Marie would emerge a stronger, wiser person if she made the right choices. Sure, some make it without an education, but for the vast majority of people, education is the key; knowledge is power.

As for the big oak tree, it still stands. Old faces may leave, but they are always replaced by new faces.

1) "She knew that forcing Betty to attend school would defeat the purpose of teaching her that the easier way out was not necessarily the best way." (p.4) Can you think of things that seem easily obtainable but are not ?

2) What are the characteristics of a true friend?

3) Do you think Gabby was a true friend to Betty? Explain.

4) Some people believe that environment determines who and what you will be in life. In what ways is this picture incorrect? Why do you think some people believe this statement?

5) Give examples of positive and negative ways to deal with anger.

6) Analyze the following statement using the information presented in Awakenings, as well as your personal knowledge. "Life involves growth and making choices."

7) We know that the choices we make for our lives will have either a positive or negative effect. Write several paragraphs about a choice that you made and the effect it had on your life.

8) When you plan an essay, you must organize your ideas in an outline. Your outline divides the essay into main ideas, subtopics, and supporting details. Write an essay on " The Hazards of Not Obtaining an Education." Use the following main ideas for your outline.

     I. Introduction
     II. Benefits of an education
     III. Hazards of not having an education
     IV. Conclusion

Information regarding purchasing the workbook may be obtained from :
Jireh Publishers
P.O. Box 99003
Norfolk, Virginia 23509-9003

.